Dead Pursuits

A NOVEL

BY

W. W. MCCULLY

Dead Pursuits
Copyright 2024 by W. W. McCully
All rights reserved

No part of this book may be reproduced in any manner including internet usage, without the written permission of the author.

This is a work of fiction. The names, characters, businesses, events and places are the imaginings of the author or are used fictitiously. Any resemblance to actual people, alive or deceased, events, and locations is coincidental.

Published by W. W. McCully
Cover by W. W. McCully

ISBN 979-8-9871010-6-3

Website
https://www.wwmccully.com

Filled with the backward march of dead pursuits and dying passions blocked by brutal beasts and collapsed dreams. The past comes alive on sleepless nights."

CHAPTER 1

Elam paused at the bedroom door before stepping over the blood pool that saturated the grimy carpet, the only spot on the floor that was clear of debris; the remainder littered with empty beer cans, take-out bags, crumpled cigarette packages, and discarded syringes. Beside the stained mattress on the floor, a nest of used condoms and their empty wrappers lay coiled in front of the plastic milk case that served as a nightstand.

The stench of the room, combined with the iron-sweet smell of the blood slowly spreading underneath the carpet, assaulted his nostrils, causing him to tug his nose and cough into his shoulder. Odor was a trigger for him, always had been, sending him reeling down a twenty-year path of auto accidents, drowning victims, drug overdoses, and welfare checks that ended with human decay. In law enforcement, the stench of feces and urine was almost commonplace, just part of the job. Decomposition and burning flesh stayed with you forever, but blood in volume was the worst – causing bile to rise to the back of his throat.

The single bulb from an overhead fixture cast a sad amber pale over the room. He swallowed hard as he pulled his flashlight and used the beam to search the dark corners and heaps of refuse to satisfy himself that nothing of importance had been overlooked. A tangle of saturated sheets and a pillowcase that had been used to stem the blood flow lay on the bed.

The girl had died here. The amount of blood loss left little doubt. His deputies had been on the scene in less than twenty minutes, but EMTs arrived almost an hour after the 911 call.

They said that she was lifeless when they got there; the body crumbled on the floor beside the bed. Her head and right shoulder extended into a dark, shallow closet that had long ago been stripped of its sliding doors – face down on a pile of cheap women's shoes.

The damned fool probably didn't intend to kill her—just blind rage. Lakin had made no attempt to flee, sitting on a couch, his forearms on his knees, in a t-shirt and shorts with a beer in his hand when deputies burst through the door. That rage had cooled, and he was submissive, even docile, his drug-clouded mind trying to deal with what he had just done and where it was going to take him.

Lakin was familiar, a repeat offender with a long history in Buford County. He was a thirty-something waste of anything and everything human who had spent most of his adult life in a series of regional correctional facilities where he learned the only skills he would ever acquire.

Outside the battered single-wide trailer, Lakin was now sitting in one of the department's few vehicles equipped for prisoner transport – slumped forward. His head against the wire and plexiglass cage that separated the front from the back seats, his homemade tattoos oozing out from the sleeves and neck of his ragged, blood-stained t-shirt.

Elam quickly calculated the man's past sins and estimated he would get at least eight years in Parchman for this one. Eight years. He wondered if he would still be sheriff in eight years. He wondered if, after the next six months of hearings, rescheduled court dates, depositions, and mental evaluations, all required before this three-time loser entered the grounds of the MDOC's prison farm in Sunflower County, would he ever have to deal with him again.

A massive figure cast a shadow from the doorway. "Boss, I'm gonna turn her loose unless you need to talk to her. Her sister is on the way to pick her up."

Elam never looked up. "Nawh – just give me the rundown."

Dolan, his chief investigator, laced his fingers across his grand belly, tucking a thumb inside his shirt. "Same ol' story. They were drinking and obviously doing meth, although she denies it. He got pissed about something, the victim got in his face, and they took to fighting. Our witness tried to get between them, and he knocked the hell out of her – threw her across the room. When she looked up, he had pulled that little 380 Taurus from somewhere and jammed it into our victim's thigh, and bam - that was it. It hit an artery and she didn't have a chance. She was unconscious by the time we got here. Called her DOA at the hospital, but she was dead long before she left here."

Elam surveyed the floor again, extending a leg and dragging his booted toe across the carpet, raking a crumpled chip bag and an empty energy drink can away from the dark and still-spreading stain.

"You know her – the witness, I mean?"

"I've dealt with her before. She's basically telling it straight—just another case of bad judgment in a long line of bad judgment. I don't think there's nothing we can charge her with unless you want to drug test her. She's got family, actually good folks."

"No. If you think her story's straight, you can let her go. Just make sure she gives us her particulars and tell her I'll want to talk to her later…. If I have to hunt her up, I'll find a reason to lock her up. Is she hurt? Does she need a doctor?"

"Couple of bruises and a stiff neck, but she won't go to the ER to be checked out. Probably afraid we'll drug test her."

Without waiting for a response, Dolan turned down the dark, narrow hallway of the mobile home to the second bedroom, where the unseen witness was sitting on an unmade bed.

Elam stepped back over the dark stain and made his way through the kitchen/living room combo that was as filthy and squalid as the bedroom. He reached the front doorway in time to watch the patrol car, with Lakin in the backseat, pull down the quarter mile-long driveway toward the county road.

He was unsure of the porch landing outside the yellow and brown trailer and stepped cautiously. Constructed of discarded two-by-fours and leveled with broken brick bats, it meshed perfectly with the forty-year-old structure: a tin can stained with oxidation and mold, insulation drooping from underneath its open sides. Propped on a series of concrete blocks and wood slabs for leveling, the 1980s model mobile home sat in the middle of what had once been a hayfield that was now overgrown in brush, weeds, and volunteer sweet gums; the yard littered with junk of all kinds.

Hell of a place to live, he thought. Even worse place to die. He'd seen a hundred others just like it across his county and knew there were thousands more: a crack house in some Detroit or Chicago slum or a blue tarp draped over a cardboard box under an overpass in any major city.

His little spot in rural America wasn't immune to the lives of people with no hope, no respect, and who no longer had a desire for dignity. When all that's gone, there isn't much left for them except to amuse themselves with drugs or any other perversion that lurks inside them.

As he walked toward his truck, he knew he could leave the cleanup of this mess to Dolan. He would take photos, search for any more weapons and drugs, seal the mobile home as a crime scene, notify any next of kin if any could be found, file the preliminary paperwork, and ensure that Lakin was properly booked into the regional correctional facility.

His office work would begin tomorrow. He would call the district attorney, field questions from local media and the television folks from the nearest station forty miles away, call for a coroner's report, which would be delayed as usual, and finally interview the suspect. He thanked God that there were no children involved in this one.

He pulled out his cell phone as he climbed into the seat of his pickup. In the glow of the screen, he checked his messages: six calls, two voicemails, and a line of text messages he didn't bother to look at. It was Friday night, school was out, it was hot and humid, and there was a full moon. It was going to be a long one.

As he pulled out of the yard, dodging piles of aluminum cans in rotting plastic bags and the skeletal remains of two old riding mowers, a call came across the radio.

One car accident on Crystal Heights Road, two miles from the intersection with Hwy 28 – one fatality and one injury – ambulance on the way. Highway Patrol has no one in the area. The first call to 911 came from a volunteer first responder. This one was his.

"This is Buford 1 - on my way but at least twenty minutes from the scene."

He stopped at the end of the drive, lit a cigarette, and cracked his window before hitting his blue lights and speeding into the darkness.

CHAPTER 2

Deeter scratched his head. His fingers came away greasy, leaving a trail across the screen of his phone as he checked again for a text message. Nothing yet.

He sat low in the seat but alert, the radio in the old Ranger playing softly. He thought he was careful. He picked this spot and had used it often before they sent him up—a spot like dozens of others scattered around Buford County, an overgrown and near-forgotten parking area between a pair of old junk cars abandoned behind a long-vacant country store.

Anybody who drove by would see another old junker. Anyone who stopped and questioned him would be told that he was looking at the rusted Impala, searching for parts, and if the law came by – well, the drugs were safely hidden outside of the Ranger. Even if they found them, they couldn't prove they belonged to him. They couldn't do anything to him but run him off..... unless they found the gun. He worried about the gun. As a convicted felon, the possession of a handgun could send him back to finish his term, but the comfort the gun brought and the cachet it gave him among his friends overrode his judgment. His dull brain simply could not grasp the inconsistency and sheer stupidity of that decision.

The light blinked on the phone – "*you there?*"

His response was short – "*waiting.*"

He scratched again and, out of habit, reached down and moved the safety forward on the 9-millimeter in the magnetic holster clutching the steering column.

The lights of a vehicle passing on the side road were barely visible through the weeds and vines. It moved slowly and then disappeared from sight. A few minutes later, it returned from the opposite direction and pulled in behind him, the headlights blinding him to anything or anyone approaching.

He cursed under his breath. Always hated dealing with new customers – "stupid sumbitches." He hesitated and considered the gun but then opened the door. He heard the crunch of gravel underneath feet as he swung out and started to rise.

The first bullet hit him in the neck, just behind the jawbone; the second caught his temple. He slumped but didn't fall, wedged between the open door and the frame. There was no look of surprise and no hint of recognition in the fading eyes frozen between the glare of the headlights and the darkness. With a slight push and twist, he fell back into the truck across the console. His head flopped over the passenger seat, and blood began to pool on the vinyl and run into the back floorboard.

It took less than a minute to remove the gun and the cell phone and do a quick search for the drugs. He pushed the body forward so that he could open the console, where he found a small bag of marijuana and a tight roll of twenties.

He hesitated for a moment before placing the dope back in the compartment. With gloved hands, he pulled the wallet from Deeter's back pocket and rummaged through it before sliding it back into the jeans.

Moments later, the second vehicle was gone, and all that remained was the soft glow of the radio and a faint rap beat matching rhythm with the blood dripping onto the seat.

***

She topped the scales at two hundred eighty pounds. The little dog at her feet, round and chubby as well, only managed five. She had fed the chihuahua, cleaned the coffee pot, and was washing the last of her breakfast dishes as she looked out the window over the sink and into the backyard.

This was the first time since his release that he hadn't come home overnight, and the old woman was worried. Things had been going so well. The boy had found some odd jobs cleaning up construction sites and even bought a few groceries. For the first time in a long time, she had some semblance of hope—hope that he would get his life straight and that she wouldn't spend the rest of her old age in a constant state of worry.

The dog pranced with his usual excitement, his untrimmed nails clicking against the hard and ancient linoleum of the kitchen floor. He spied a fruit gnat rising from a bowl full of apples and bananas on the counter, leading to incessant barking and low growls as he followed it as best he could, jumping on a cabinet door as the gnat landed on the counter's edge.

"Shut up, Toot."

The woman grabbed a wooden spoon from the drainboard and took a light swing at the dog. He growled and took a position under the cheap metal dining table, where he continued to bark.

She turned back to look out the window again, praying to see a white Ranger pulling into its usual parking spot on the mix of gravel and grass behind the carport.

With all the grace of a sixty-two-year-old obese woman with bad knees, she made her way to the living room, the last cup of coffee in her hand. Fox News was reporting on a train derailment in the upper Midwest as she fell into her recliner, the dog jumping into her lap and burrowing himself into her folds hidden underneath her house dress.

That boy was all she had left—nothing else in this world. She could make it on her disability check, everything she owned was paid for, and she even had a little money put aside from last year's timber sale on the last twenty acres of the old place.

She was there for him. She was always there for him, and in her old age, nothing else occupied her mind. Get him on his feet and get him leveled off. Maybe he could even find himself a girl if he'd just stay out of trouble.

A buxom blonde woman was pointing at a weather map of the Northeast as she turned the volume down low on the TV so she could hear if he pulled into the drive.

CHAPTER 3

The courthouse was old but not historic or of any architectural significance. The three-story red brick structure sat inside the square of downtown Seymore, Mississippi, surrounded on all sides by row buildings: some empty, some with law and CPA offices, a diner, an old hardware store, a pharmacy, and more knickknack and gift shops than a town twice its size could support.

The building had never been seriously remodeled since it was built in the 1950s to replace the historic structure that had burned to the ground on a cold New Year's Eve. A few coats of interior paint, wiring upgrades to accommodate twenty-first-century technology, and a 1990s elevator workover required to meet ADA standards were the extent of its modernization.

The Sheriff's office was on the lowest level, half buried in the Mississippi red clay. Thompson and his officers had their own entrance, partially shielded by a long, narrow metal building that housed a patrol car that needed significant repair before it could be sold at auction, a pair of ATVs used for search and rescue, and a john boat with a thirty-five-horse Johnson outboard that was occasionally required when a creek or watershed needed to be dragged for a drowning victim.

Sheriff Elam Thompson sat between the buildings, hidden from the windows of the courthouse's upper floors. He perched on one of the wooden benches built by a former trustee for the sole purpose of providing a place where courthouse smokers could sit and feed their addiction.

Thompson was on his second cigarette, waiting for the prison transport to arrive with Lakin. He resented having to leave his office to smoke, but it was a compromise grudgingly accepted since the city had passed a non-smoking ordinance to receive a small federal grant. He never liked the fact that a city ordinance could apply to a county building, but a few busybodies on the second and third floors had applauded the effort. After a round of contentious words, the smokers and non-smokers had reached some sort of truce.

Officially, they weren't supposed to smoke here either; too close to the entrance to the building, but that was part of the compromise. They wouldn't be pushed any further. Since this entrance was only used by his department and the others didn't have to see the clouds of white-grey smoke rising at intervals throughout the day, they turned a blind eye to keep the peace.

Thompson rolled the half-smoked generic between his fingers, reviewing the morning's events in his head. The district attorney had decided on a first-degree murder charge that would certainly be pled down to second or even manslaughter if Lakin could afford a decent lawyer. The victim had little family, and nobody would squawk too much about a reduced charge.

As expected, the coroner's report wouldn't be completed for days or even weeks—not that it mattered much. The whole case was cut and dried, but it would still take six months or more to work its way through a broken and undermanned legal system.

The local court system was clogged just like the larger jurisdictions: lack of money, huge caseloads, too many appeals, and legal wranglings. Here, there were fewer cases but fewer courtrooms and full-time district attorneys and investigators to process them.

He had pulled Lakin's file that morning and found everything he expected: a string of drug charges, assaults, possession of a firearm by a convicted felon, and a couple of domestic abuse charges on two different women. He'd been a suspect in a couple of shootings, but because they were drug-related, those didn't go anywhere. When drugs were involved, and they were always involved, no one talked. Lakin's name was one of about twenty that appeared regularly on court dockets, one of twenty that were involved in half the crimes in Buford County.

He flicked the cigarette at a drywall bucket full of sand that served as the county ashtray. The butt bounced off the side and lay on the concrete patio amongst a dozen or so others, still smoldering. He reached into his pocket for the pack of smokes and tapped out another just as the heavy metal door leading into his office opened.

Lindon, the old dispatcher, leaned out as he brushed at his shirt, scattering crumbs from the sheet cake purchased at the bake sale up the street by some appreciative citizen.

"Got a call, Sheriff. Says she'll only talk to you – missing person."

"Who is it?"

"Arlene Deeter."

"She the caller or the missing person?"

"She's the one on the phone."

He sighed heavily and put the pack back in his shirt pocket. "God help us! Problems poppin' up like mushrooms on a manure pile." He dropped the loose cigarette back into his shirt pocket.

"Tell Dolan when he gets here with Lakin to take him into his office and I'll be there when I can."

Thompson rose with some effort and shuffled to the door; the back of his hand pressed against the small of his back as he walked stiffly inside.

***

The old lady was loud and agitated. He held the phone a few inches from his ear. "No, ma'am. We haven't had any trouble with him since he's been back. We don't deal with him, though; he reports to his parole officer."

The phone cord crossed his belly, his feet propped on his tired metal desk, a desk continually covered with booking sheets, old newspapers, and printed emails. A small dough-colored stress ball and a handful of nine-millimeter shells sat beside the phone. Over the line, he could hear a small dog yapping in the background.

"When's the last time you saw him?"

"Bout four o'clock yesterday." Thompson could hear the anxiety in her voice. "He's been real good since he got back – had some jobs, comes in at decent hours, and been real respectful. This ain't like him."

"How old is he now – twenty-one – twenty-two?"

"He's twenty-three. I'm real worried, Sheriff. He won't answer his phone, and I ain't got no cell phone to text him. I'm telling you – this just ain't like him."

"Well, I'll tell everybody to be on the lookout for him. He drives an old white Ford Ranger, doesn't he?"

"Yes, sir. He's got one of those vulgar things on his rear window—you know, the one with a little kid peeing on a Chevy."

"You know his license number? Is it registered to him or you?"

It's in my name, but I don't remember the license. I could probably find it, though."

"That's alright, we'll look it up. But I have to tell you there's not much official I can do yet. He's an adult, and he hasn't been gone all that long. He's probably still asleep on somebody's couch. Probably call you in a while. But we'll keep our eyes open. If we find him, we'll send him home."

The old woman on the other end of the phone paused a bit and murmured an insincere thank you before hanging up.

Thompson tapped a few keys on the old dusty computer on his desk, got a license number, and hand-scribbled a note to give to his dispatcher to issue to any deputies on patrol. He considered sending it to the police departments in Seymore and Coyville but decided it wasn't urgent enough yet.

Local BOLO only
Jason Deeter, aka Joe Dirt, 23

White male

White 97 Ford Ranger plate # BFU136

Not seen since Friday afternoon – if seen – tell him to call his granny. – no charges.

He realized that he should have taken down the man's cell number and asked about his friends, but a twenty-something ex-con who wouldn't call his granny was not a major priority right now. He knew, ninety-nine percent of the time, these guys would reappear after they sobered up or crashed after a binge. Granny would take him in, give him a place to lick his wounds, and make excuses for him until he repeated the whole damned thing over again or till he messed up bad enough to be sent back to finish his time.

He grabbed the note and headed across the hall to the cubicle where his dispatcher fielded daily calls about loose dogs, loud trucks, and suspicious vehicles.

Lindon was leaning forward in his chair, listening intently to a caller as he watched Thompson lay the note on the desk. He held up his hand to hold the Sheriff's attention.

"Hold on. The Sheriff just walked in. I'm gonna put you on speakerphone. Repeat what you just told me."

The voice on the other end sounded aged and deep country. "I said there's a car in the creek. Looks like it run off the road. Ain't nothin' stickin' up but a little bit of the back end."

Elam's shoulders slumped as he looked at Lindon. "Sir, this is Sheriff Thompson. Who am I speaking to, and where is this at?"

"Elam, this is Lucas Minfield. The car's in Leechee Creek at the bridge on Pearl Crossing Road. Looks like it might a been there a day or two."

"Can you tell if anybody's in it?"

"Hell, Elam, you know that creek's so muddy, Peter couldn't find his pecker in there. I'll tell you this, though, if there was somebody in that thing, they didn't get out – not the way she's sitting in the water."

"Alright, Mr. Minfield, if you would, just sit tight. We're on our way. I might need to talk to you."

Lindon disconnected the call and looked up curiously. "Who the hell is Peter?"

Thompson shook his head. He had ceased to be amused by Lindon's literal nature and no longer found it amusing.

"Call Jimmy and have him meet me there. Tell him he's probably going to get wet. Then call the next wrecker service on rotation and send them out there."

Thompson walked back to his office to pick up an extra pack of cigarettes and grab his cell phone. As he headed out the door, he looked back at Lindon. "Tell Dolan to get Lakin's statement. If I need to, I'll talk to him later – and get John Luke to come and hook up the boat and bring it out in case we have to search the creek."

Lindon looked at him flatly. "John Luke's not on duty."

"Well, he is now."

CHAPTER 4

Thompson left the downtown square and drove down tree-lined Fitz Street to the intersection with the highway headed south. It was a twenty-five-mile drive to the location on Pearl Crossing Road, first down the state highway and then across country on a series of narrow asphalt and gravel roads.

He picked up the radio and called back to Lindon."This is Buford1"

"Go ahead, Sheriff."

Have we had any stolen vehicle reports in the last week or so?"

"Just one—last Sunday night. Hang on, let me look ….. It was a Chevy Silverado, only about six months old."

"Alright, text me the particulars on it, just in case this is it."

Minfield didn't say what kind of vehicle it was, but a new, expensive truck would be typical of insurance fraud. A man gets enthralled with bells and whistles, a slick salesman massages his ego, and he buys more truck than he can afford. Soon, he gets upside down on the loan and can't or won't make the payments, reports it stolen, and it ends up wrecked or in a creek like this. It was a good chance, that's exactly what happened here. He hoped so. He didn't relish fishing a body out of a mud creek.

His jaw was set hard, and he had recently developed a habit of grinding his teeth. He lit another cigarette and called his wife, leaving her a voicemail stating that, once again, he wouldn't be home on a Saturday afternoon.

He was in the first year of a second term. At forty-two, he already felt old. The stress of last year's campaign, the incessant politics, the lack of funding for his department, and the explosion of drugs across the area had made him prematurely gray.

Twenty extra pounds that came with the job, the lack of exercise and sleep had begun to take a toll on his body. At his last checkup in February, he was warned he was headed for trouble. A family history of heart problems and cancer hung over him, and the doctor was convinced he had sleep apnea as well. He felt he shouldn't have to deal with these problems at his age, so he continued to ignore them.

He turned off the state highway onto a feeder that would lead to Pearl Crossing Road, which ran southwest. Except for the purpose, the drive was a pleasant one: two-lane country roads lined with planted pine plantations, most nearing maturity, and bottoms of hardwood oak and hickory, with an occasional farmstead tucked among the trees or along the edge of small pastures.

It was hot, but the full summer heat and humidity had not arrived yet. He rolled his window down to allow the smoke to escape and provide fresh air.

Pearl Crossing eventually dead-ended near the county line in the small community of Church Hill. Founded not long after the Civil War by freed slaves, Church Hill had grown and prospered. By the 1950s, it was home to two churches, Methodist and Missionary Baptist, a small country store, and a meeting hall that served for dances and family gatherings.

By the late '60s, social changes and the decline of the surrounding farms had begun to take their toll on the population. The country store was closed and was now choked by weeds and trash. The meeting hall had been torn down for scrap lumber, and the Methodist Church was now abandoned—damaged by a tornado in 83'. It had never been repaired.

Leechee Creek crossed the road two miles from Church Hill, running in a southeasterly direction before joining the headwaters of the Pearl River. The road curved just before reaching the creek, and he was almost upon it when he saw three vehicles and a pair of ATVs pulled to the side of the old wooden span.

His newest deputy, Jimmy Smith, stood on the bridge with an older black man Elam recognized as Luther Monroe, and two teenage boys. They were looking over the north side, down into the slow swirling water—the two boys leaning on the rail. Lucas Minfield, the man who made the report, was sitting in the driver's seat of his old Chevy with the door open.

Thompson pulled around and parked in the middle of the bridge. As he got out, Minfield started walking toward the rest of the group.

"What we got, Jimmy?"

An ex-Marine, Jimmy Smith fit the image of a modern law enforcement officer. Young and fit with a military tattoo on one bicep, short blonde hair, and a pleasant but strong face, he wore the base summer uniform of the Buford County Department – short black sleeves and blue jeans over a pair of polished cowboy boots.

"Don't know yet. I just got here myself."

Thompson leaned over the creosote rail. The vehicle had nosedived off the steep bank to the right of the bridge and twisted slightly so that only the left side of a rear fender was exposed. The license plate would be just a few inches under the muddy water. It was definitely not a truck.

Thompson turned to shake hands with the tall black man with a shock of white hair. "Mr. Monroe, how are you, sir?"

The man nodded and took his hand. "That don't look good, does it?'

"No sir, it don't – Y'all ain't missing anybody, are you?"

"No sir, ever-body down our way is where they supposed to be – at least as far as I know."

Luther Monroe was a deacon in the local Missionary Baptist Church. He was a good man and a leader in the community who knew everyone and their business but had the dignity and care to keep most of it to himself. He took a seat on the bridge railing and crossed his hands in front of him. His flat expression indicated that he had nothing more to say.

By this time, Lucas Minfield had reached them and pointed at the kids. "These two boys here are the ones who found it."

Thompson glanced at the two – thirteen, fourteen-year-olds at the most. The bigger of the two, looking at the ground and moving gravel with his toe. The younger looked the men straight in the eye, excited and eager to talk.

"How'd you happen to see this, boys?"

The younger one took the lead. "We rode up here on our four-wheelers—we wuz gonna go fishin'. When we saw that stickin' out, we knew it wasn't there last week, so we rode down to Mr. Minfield's and told him about it."

"Well, you did good, boys. Did you see anybody around here the last few days, any strangers, I mean?"

"No sir, but we been in vacation bible school all week. We ain't had a chance to come up here for a few days."

"You got anything to add, son?" Thompson spoke directly to the older boy.

"He never looked up and mumbled, "No sir, we wuz just trying to go fishin."

Thompson walked to the northeast corner of the bridge with Jimmy. "Mr. Minfield, could you move your truck to the other side so I can get a good look at where he went off the road."

Minfield walked back to his truck without responding, backed up a few feet, and moved to the south side of the road by the bridge.

Thompson walked fifty feet back from the bridge and could easily see the tracks of the vehicle in the tall grass as it left the road. There was a gentle slope at first, then an eight-foot drop to the creek. He walked down the incline to get a better look, Jimmy following behind. The exposed maroon fender was only about twenty feet from him as he stood on the edge of the bank.

"Maybe a Nissan?"

"Yeah, that's what I thought too. Probably an older model Altima. Any reports on one or anybody missing?"

"Not like this. I've got a wrecker that's supposed to be on its way. Call and see where it's at. You may have to go back to the intersection and bring them here in case they get lost."

Thompson and Jimmy walked back to the roadway. There would be no skid marks on a gravel road, and it hadn't rained in more than a week, so it was unlikely the driver had lost control in a patch of mud. Most likely drunk or high – or even better yet, maybe this was a stolen car from another county.

He was inclined to make the boys leave the scene, knowing that something might be coming out of that creek that their young eyes didn't need to see. He stopped and decided against it. If he ran them off, they'd tell everyone in Church Hill, and within thirty minutes, there would be a crowd to contend with. Instead, he told them to move their ATVs to the other side of the bridge and stay there beside them.

By the time the wrecker reached the bridge, the stubs of half a pack of cigarettes had found their way down Leechee Creek. Thompson didn't know the driver – must be a new hand. The patch on his blue work shirt indicated that his name was Tony. Tony looked nervously at the tracks running off the slope into the creek.

Thompson stood on the wrecker's running board and leaned into the window. "There's a driveway about a quarter mile past the bridge. Turn around, come back, and park right here."

Tony didn't respond at first, then nodded and said, "It's in the creek? I ain't going in no water."

Thompson replied, 'You won't have to. That's our job," grinning at the young deputy standing nearby.

The hookup took another twenty minutes. Jimmy walked down to the creek's edge and stripped off his shirt, socks, and boots. Thompson pulled a rope from his gearbox in the back of his truck and tied it to the bridge rail. He moved out from the bridge and held the rope behind his back as he belayed the deputy down the steepest part of the bank and into the muddy water.

Jimmy was careful not to jump between the car and the bank but entered the water on the upstream side of the vehicle. He put his hands on the fender and pushed to see how stable the car's position was. Satisfied, he moved closer and began searching underwater at the rear of the car for a place on the frame to connect the cable from the wrecker.

"You touchin' bottom?"

Jimmy looked up in disgust, his face wet from the splashing and the sweat. "Hell no. I'm standing on the rear tire right now."

Two minutes later, he had found the frame and securely attached the cable spooled from the back of the wrecker. "Got it. Now get me outta here!"

He climbed up the steep bank, untied the rope around his waist, picked up his boots and shirt, and walked gingerly up the remaining slope before sitting on the tailgate of the Sheriff's truck.

Thompson walked back onto the bridge so he could watch safely and pointed to Tony – "Alright, let's go."

The line tightened slowly, taking in any slack. The car moved toward the bank and slowly began to creep upward. The license plate—a local plate—was now exposed.

"Damn," Thompson muttered under his breath.

By this time, Jimmy had replaced his socks and boots and joined the other men on the bridge, using his shirt to dry off his upper torso. The car continued to creep upward, sliding against the steep bank.

Thompson shouted, "Hold it right there for a minute. Let's let some of that water drain out and take some of the weight off that cable."

Water was streaming out from around the doors and sloshing through the rear windows that were half lowered.

After a few moments, Thompson walked back to the wrecker and gave the operator some added instructions before walking down the slope and positioning himself well to the right of the cable as the car began to move again.

The maroon Altima was fully exposed now, and muddy water continued to stream out in all directions. The rear tires cleared the bank, and the car slowly tilted back. When the front tires cleared the bank by a few feet, Thompson waved to the operator, and the car stopped.

After most of the water drained from the driver's side door, Thompson walked up and grabbed the latch. The door opened easily as the last of the water splashed to the ground and out the floorboard. He stood in the open doorway, blocking the view of the others on the bridge.

"Hold it right there. Jimmy, get your camera - we got a body."

***

A body submerged in water for a period of time is the stuff of nightmares. This one would haunt Thompson's dreams for a while. Slumped across the front seat and console, head in the passenger's floorboard, there was no way to view the face without moving the body. Jimmy took pictures of the inside of the car and the body while Thompson stood behind him. "Alright, now step back; take a few of the car and the area where it went in the creek."

Thompson began giving more instructions: "Run that tag, and let's see who this car belongs to – and send those kids home. Tell them this is now a crime scene, and they can't be around here. Then call the coroner and tell him to get here now – no excuses. Tell him he'll need to bring a hearse from his funeral home. We're going to drag the car up to the road, and then you and I are going to take a look at this fellow. And find out where John Luke is with that boat."

They climbed back up to the road, and Jimmy began to follow his instructions as Thompson watched the wrecker slowly drag the Altima to a level spot on the side of the road.

"You want me to load it, Sheriff?"

Thompson looked at the operator. "Not yet, Tony – we got a body in there. It's gonna be awhile."

"Lord Jesus! A body? Good God! You know who it is?"

"Not yet. Just don't touch the car or move it anymore until we get through here."

"Yes, sir. I ain't touchin' nothin'."

He paused and ran his fingers through his hair. "Sheriff, you may have to call RayRay. I gotta couple of other calls he was expecting me to make. Looks like this could take all afternoon."

"It could at that. I'll square it with RayRay."

"Lord Jesus!"

Thompson walked to the passenger side of the Altima. This door opened easily as well. The body had not moved significantly in the climb up the slope. A pale white arm lay over the face. He was young, maybe even a teenager—wearing baggy jeans and a t-shirt that was once white but now pale brown from the muddy water.

"Jimmy, bring a pair of gloves when you come."

Jimmy had already started toward the vehicle. He wheeled around, searched behind the seat of his pickup, and produced a box of blue surgical gloves.

"Don't forget the camera."

He wheeled around again and grabbed the camera from the driver's seat.

The two men stood beside the car as the deputy took photos of the gruesome scene in the front seat. They were solemn and preparing themselves for the next step in the process when they were startled by a thumping and flapping sound coming from the back floorboard.

Jimmy stepped back – "What the hell was that?"

The Sheriff managed a wry smile and reached to open the rear door of the Altima. Jimmy cautiously peered into the rear area of the car. In the floorboard, still flopping and mouthing for air, were at least a half dozen catfish, the largest approaching five pounds.

"Well, I'll be…"

"You wanna take 'em home for supper?" Thompson said.

The thought of a fish fry made the bile churn in Jimmy's stomach, and he stepped away from the car, his hands on his knees.

"Yellow"

"What?"

Yellow cat. Bullhead, actually. They're in the creeks and rivers around here, but you don't see them much in lakes and ponds."

Thompson waited to see if the young deputy would puke his guts out. "We'll have to get them outta there before we haul the car off. They'll make a hell of a stink in a day or two."

He turned his attention back to the corpse on the front floorboard. Snapping on his gloves, he reached down and moved the arm to expose the face. It was a young face with soft features and closely cropped brown hair – it was almost peaceful, almost angelic, except for the two small round holes just above and behind the ear.

"Well, that changes things considerably."

He pointed out the wounds to Jimmy who now stood behind him. The deputy remained silent and began snapping photos again.

Thompson's eye poured over the car – "Keys are in the ignition, and it's in neutral. I don't see a cell phone, but it could be under the body or in his pocket. Lift him up."

The deputy looked at him with a mixture of dread and disbelief.

Elam growled, "Put the camera down, grab him under the arms, and lift him into the seat. He's dead – he ain't gonna bite ya. I need to see if there's anything under him."

The deputy bent into a crouch, leaned into the car, and turned his head away, his face pale and hard, before lifting the body into a sitting position on the seat. In the process, a small cloth wallet fell to the floor. Thompson flipped it open, the driver's license in the front plastic sleeve.

"Jason Dean, age 26. Know him?"

Jimmy thought for a moment. "Yeah, don't know if he's got a record, but we've stopped him a time or two. Seemed to always be in the wrong place at the wrong time, but we never were able to charge him for anything serious. Hell, I never would have recognized him."

"A couple of days underwater tends to do that to you. Definitely in the wrong place this time."

Jimmy paused, lost in the grimness of the scene, and then seemed to gather himself. "I forgot to tell you. The car is registered to Denise Mayfair. Lindon says he thinks she works at the hospital."

"Know if there's a relation?"

"Not right off hand, but somebody will know."

Thompson stared into the face, drained of any color or life. "Not much more we can do till the coroner gets here. Get something and throw it over him in case somebody drives by... and don't put the name out over the radio. Everybody and his brother listens to that damn thing now – don't want the family finding out like that."

Thompson walked to his truck and dug through the backseat. He returned with a plastic garbage bag and an old wooden billy club. Taking care not to be finned, he raked the catfish into the bag, returned to the middle of the bridge, and dumped them over the side under the watchful eyes of Luther Monroe and Lucas Minfield.

Wadding up the bag in one hand, he stood stiff-legged next to the rail, turned to the men, and said, "Gentlemen, this is now a crime scene. I'm short of deputies, as you can see. I was hoping that one of you would go back to the last intersection and watch for the coroner or any of my folks and direct them down this way. If the other of you would direct any traffic and hurry along any rubberneckers until my other deputies arrive."

The men agreed, little expression on their faces. Minfield headed to his truck to work the intersection, and Monroe took a position at the far end of the bridge. Neither asked any questions but both took a hard look at the Altima covered in mud and creek sand.

Thompson went back to his truck and sat on the tailgate, lit a cigarette, and began making a mental list of things that had to be done:

    Get the coroner's signature
    Bag the body
    Get it to the State Medical Examiner's Office in Jackson
    Search the vehicle
    Tow the car to the auto shop at the prison and seal it
    Make a decision to drag the creek
    Get the State Crime Lab involved
    Find the next of kin and inform them
    Start questioning folks in the area
    Look for cell phone records
    Question his friends and family
    Buy another carton of cigarettes and call his wife again

The address on the license noted an older residential area of modest homes in north Seymore. He picked up his phone and checked the signal – two bars. He punched a speed dial and heard Lindon's voice on the other end of the line.

"You got an address on this Mayfair woman?"

Lindon had the same address as the one on the driver's license.

"Ask around the courthouse; call the hospital personnel department if you have to. Find out if she's got a kid, grandson, or live-in by the name of Jason Dean—but don't tell them anything else."

"Got it, Boss. I'll call you back in a few."

***

It was 1:00 pm before the coroner arrived and 1:30 before the body was in transit to Jackson. During that time, he got the rundown on Denise Mayfair: forty-three, divorced, no kids, but she had a nephew named Jason.

She was working the seven to three weekend shift at the hospital. If he left now, he could still catch her at work and maybe find her clergy and some coworkers to help soften the news.

By this time, a second deputy, John Luke, had arrived with the departmental boat in tow; his surliness abated by his curiosity over the crime scene. He and Jimmy stood by the Altima, gloved and waiting for the go-ahead to search the vehicle. All four doors now stood open, creek water still dripping from the undercarriage.

Thompson motioned to the two deputies and walked down the bank to issue instructions. "If I leave now, I can catch the next of kin at work. Jimmy, call Dolan and have him come down and take over the investigation. I'm working that guy to death, but I don't have much choice. Now that the body's gone, I think we can let Mr. Minfield and Mr. Monroe go about their business. Ya'll start interviewing anybody within a mile or so of here after you search the car. I know I don't have to tell you, but I will anyway – bag and mark anything you find, no matter how small or unimportant it seems. Tell Dolan I'll call him as soon as I can."

Together, they walked back up the bank, and Thompson crawled into the pickup. He cranked it, paused, and leaned out the window. "When you're through, and Dolan gives the okay, have them tow the car to the prison shop." He lit the last cigarette in the pack, crossed the bridge, turned around, and headed toward town, cell phone in hand.

CHAPTER 5

Denise Mayfair knew that something was seriously wrong. As her shift ended, she was called to the hospital's human resources office. Her coworker, Mary Barnstead, and an older black Methodist minister who served as a grief counseling chaplain flanked the hospital administrator sitting behind a desk.

"What's going on?" she said, looking from one face to another.

The administrator, Ed Lang, stared at his hands as he spoke. "The Sheriff called here. He's coming by to talk to you."

"What's wrong? Is something wrong at my house? Did I do something?' Fear and a touch of anger moved across her face.

The man shrugged. "I'm not sure, but he should be here any minute. Mary, why don't you get Denise a bottle of water from the break room while we wait."

Mary returned almost at once, followed by Thompson. After doing this more than a hundred times, he had learned that it was best to get right to it.

"Mrs. Mayfair, do you have a family member by the name of Jason Dean?"

She nodded slightly.
"I'm sorry to tell you this………"

She didn't look surprised. In a sense, she seemed almost relieved, as if this were something expected, which was at least better than what wasn't expected until she learned the manner of her nephew's death. That shook her. This was a death that was hard to imagine, hard to forget, hard to accept.

She swallowed deeply, dread in her eyes. "Do I…Do I need to identify the body?"

"No, ma'am. He's already on the way to the crime lab." Thompson paused, giving her a few moments to absorb the information. "I know now is not the time, but when you're able, I do need to get some information from you. It can wait until later. I'm sure there's some family that you need to contact."

She was silent momentarily, her eyes downcast, her chin almost touching her chest. "No family; ain't nobody to call."

Her hand trembled slightly as she moved it across her forehead. "Damn, I need a smoke."

The administrator shifted in his chair uncomfortably. The hospital had a strict no-smoking policy—not even on the grounds. "I suppose no one would object if you went outside, away from the doors…under the circumstances."

Thompson gave him a hard look. The woman was struggling, dealing with shock, and this bureaucrat was worried about cigarette smoke.

He turned to the woman, "I have a fresh pack in my truck. You take a few minutes with your friend and the

Reverend here, and I'll be outside waiting for you." Thompson walked to the door, giving the man behind the desk one more look of disdain.

He sat in the truck listening to the chatter on the radio, air conditioning at half blast with the window halfway down. An abandoned car report and a report of a suspicious character near an abandoned house had come across since he sat down. He watched as Denise Mayfair exited the double glass doors and walked uncertainly toward him.

An attractive woman, he thought. About his age, but he couldn't remember her from school. She looked older than forty-three. He could tell life had been hard on her. There were lines on her still-young face that shouldn't have been there, and she carried extra weight in her hips.

He lifted the latch and pushed the passenger door open for her. As she climbed in, he offered her the pack of cigarettes.

Sorry, but generics are all I've got – bout all I can afford."

"Believe me, I know." She took his offer of a light and inhaled deeply. "Do you mind if we drive? I gotta get away from this place for a bit."

Somewhat relieved, he left the parking lot and headed away from town. "So, you're the only family?"

'Yeah." She took another long inhale and stared out the side window. "At least so you can tell. His mom, my sister, died of cancer almost ten years ago—his Dad – who knows where the hell he is. Last I heard, he was on the Coast working in a casino. I got a number for him, but I doubt it's good. We ain't heard from him in more than two years. I was Jason's guardian till he turned eighteen, but I couldn't do much with him."

"So, he lived with you?"

"Well, he used my address, but he hasn't really lived there in a couple of years. I found some weed and some pills on my kitchen table one morning. He was passed out on the sofa, and I flushed it all. He got mad and left and never came back except for a night or two when he was broke or hiding out from somebody he owed money to."

"Was there somebody in particular he seemed afraid of, or did he mention who he owed money to?"

She clenched her fists and rolled her eyes. "Sheriff, I don't know. He didn't tell me anything; he didn't want me to know anything. I hadn't seen him in more than two weeks. He avoided me mostly – he owed me for that car. The car – I guess it's totaled?"

"Yes, ma'am. I'm afraid so. It's been underwater for a couple of days."

"Damn! The insurance has lapsed. I just got the notice this week. He was supposed to pay for it. I was going to call him when I got off this afternoon."

They were almost ten miles out when he took a country road to the south, intent on making a long loop that would eventually lead them back to the hospital. She took another cigarette from the pack on the seat, and he handed her the lighter.

"I guess I must seem cold to you, but I'm not. I just couldn't do it anymore. Didn't seem like there was anything I could do to reach him. He was a grown man. At some point, you just give up."

She cracked the window to allow the smoke that had built up inside the cab to escape. "I knew he'd end up like this – not murdered maybe, but I figured I'd get a call one night, a car wreck or an overdose."

"So, you knew he was using something stronger than pot?"

"Oh yeah. I didn't know what it was for sure. I assumed meth. That's the drug of choice around here, ain't it?"

"Yeah, usually. White kids do meth, and the black kids usually do crack, although that's changing some. Occasionally, we see some ecstasy, some prescription stuff, and lately, we've even seen some heroin."

She sat silent for a few moments, in thought and choosing her words carefully. "He asked me about some meds once- since I worked in the hospital. I guess he thought I could walk into the pharmacy and help myself. I couldn't believe he asked me that. That's when I knew he was beyond anything I could help him with."

"What was he asking about -anything particular?"

"Not really. I think he just mentioned names he knew - Valium and hydrocodone, but I think he was just fishin' for a fix of anything."

"Do you know where he stayed?"

"I don't think he had a place of his own. I think he just crashed wherever he could. Although a couple of times, one of the ladies who works in the nursing home said she saw his car, my car parked at a house down on Orangefield Road. I just assumed it was a buddy's of his or a drug house."

"What about friends? Did you know any of them?"

"He didn't bring anybody around – not since he was in high school. Never saw him with any girls, never saw him hanging out. There was a guy who came by the house with him a few months back. Jason wanted to borrow some money, and this guy just stood in the living room by the door. Never introduced him or said his name; a tall, pale, skinny kid with a big mop of red hair – looked like a kitchen match. Seemed harmless."

"Anybody else that we might could talk to?"

"Sheriff, we just didn't hang out in the same circles. I get up in the morning, go to work, come home, watch TV, and go to bed. I ain't been in a bar or to a concert or movie in ten years. Hell, I ain't been to church in five. If I don't work with them or live next door to them, I don't see them."

As she stubbed out the second cigarette, she reached for a third, still in possession of his lighter. "I don't know what to do now," she said softly as she looked out the side window at the green cow pastures and country homes with broad porches that lined the narrow asphalt road winding back toward town.

"You got somebody you can call – somebody to stay with you tonight?"

"That ain't what I meant. I don't know who to call about taking care of everything. I ain't got no money for a funeral, and I wouldn't even know where to look to see if Jason had any. How do I get the body back? You know, I hear that TV commercial that says a funeral can cost $10,000. Ain't no way I can do that."

He saw tears for the first time as she wiped them away with the back of her hand. "It's not as bad as all that. Legally, you're not obligated to take care of anything, although most folks do. It'll be several days before the medical examiner releases his body. Go by one of the funeral homes on Monday morning and explain the situation to them. They can arrange to transport the body back if you want, and they can help you make some reasonable arrangements. Probably let you pay over time if you need to. They're good folks and know how to handle all this."

She grew silent and stared out the window as he turned the truck back onto the main highway. Despite the hard shell that comes with years on the job, he felt sympathy for her, knowing the grief, the financial issues, and the questions she would face in the coming days. Like most folks with a hard life and hard problems, she had probably created most of them, but not this one. This one had been foisted upon her, and she would have to find a way to bear it as best she could.

He thought of the sense of guilt that would inevitably come to her—guilt fostered by the relief she would feel when she realized she no longer had to tamp down her fear and uncertainty every time the phone rang or her wayward nephew showed up at her door.

He'd seen that guilt countless times: the guilt of a caregiver upon the death of an Alzheimer's patient or an invalid, the guilt of a parent who spent years and fortunes on a child whose addictions or mental illness led to a sad fate in the back room of a drug house. That uncertainty, that stress and fear now dissipated, bringing relief that could only generate guilt from its presence.

He handed her a tissue and the pack of cigarettes as he entered the hospital drive.

CHAPTER 6

After he delivered Mayfair to her car parked in the employees' parking lot, he called Dolan. His truck was idling, and the air conditioning was now on full blast.

"I screwed up. I didn't call MHP for a portable crime lab. We first thought it was an accident, and then I got in too big of a hurry."

Dolan's voice was reassuring. "I got you covered. When Jimmy called me and told me the situation, I stopped them from searching the vehicle and called MIB. Lucky, cause the tech on call this weekend just happened to be in our district. He's here now."

Thompson was relieved. He'd seen too many cases lost because of sloppy evidence handling. Some didn't even make it to trial. "Did y'all find a phone?"

"No phone. Roach clip in the console and maybe a half-ounce of weed in a baggie stuffed between the seats, but in the trunk …. well, let's just say he was running a corner drug store."

"Yeah… what exactly?"

"Not sure exactly. In the well under the spare tire, we found some bags. One had opened, and it was just a melted mess of stuff. The other had a dozen pill bottles. Looks like all prescription stuff. I recognize the oxycodone and the Valium, but there are at least five or six different kinds of drugs. Maybe some Adderall, Vicodin, other stuff I don't know, but there's a lot of it."

"Damned strange. You know he had a phone. Strange they would take the phone and not take the drugs."

"Maybe they didn't know about the drugs, maybe they got scared off, or maybe they didn't care. Could be this had nothing to do with the drugs."

Thompson doubted it. Almost everything bad that happened in this county had to do with drugs or alcohol. The problems had exploded in the last twenty years as gang connections developed and a flood of Mexican meth had replaced the local production.

"The front windows were up, and the back windows were only open a few inches. It's not likely the phone's in the creek unless they threw it in there. I don't think it makes much sense to search for it. Between the mud and the current, it would be all but impossible to find, even if it were there. But I'll leave the decision up to you. It doesn't seem likely there was anybody else in the car. The way it was sealed, I don't believe a body could've floated out of it. Anyway, one missing person that nobody's looking for is one thing – two would be unusual."

Dolan agreed. "Don't see much use dragging that creek for a body when there's no evidence it exists."

Thompson thought for a moment and then said, "There's no need to drag the creek, but have Jimmy and John Luke walk the banks downstream for a couple hundred yards. If there is a body or some evidence, it might be hung up on a snag or in a curve. It's best we cover all the bases."

"Yes, sir, Boss."

"I ain't got much on this end. Doesn't seem to be a place of residence for this kid. Might have been staying at a house out on Orangefield Road, probably the Camfield place, and has been seen in the company of a tall, skinny, redheaded white kid."

"That ain't much."

"Nope. That ain't much."

Thompson was tired – bone tired: thirty-six hours with little sleep, two murder cases, and a next of kin death notice. Any adrenalin produced was ebbing from his body. "I'm going home to get some sleep and see my kid. Call me if anything new comes up."

Dolan said, "One other thing before you go. Jimmy talked to an old lady who lives on Pearl Crossing. Kind of a busybody. Says she ain't got air conditioning, so she sits on her porch in the afternoon. Anyway, she said on Wednesday, just before dark, she saw a red car and late model Ford F150, gray or charcoal, going down the road toward Church Hill. Said she noticed cause both of the drivers looked white and just about everybody down that way is black. She couldn't describe them – just said they were white."

"Not much help. There's gotta be a couple of hundred gray F150's in this county. Alright, I'm outta here."

He ended the call and looked across the lot as he reversed out of his parking space. Among the boxy sedans and SUVs were a pair of F150s—one silver gray, the other charcoal. He pulled out a business card as he slowly cruised behind them and wrote down the tag numbers. What the hell? He had nothing else to go on. He reached for another pack of cigarettes before he realized that Denise Mayfair still had his lighter.

CHAPTER 7

She lay on a bed that hadn't been made in weeks, on sheets that hadn't been washed in weeks, and a pillow between her knees. Her brain was on fire. The pills didn't seem to do much anymore, and her supply was getting low.

A fifth of white rum sat on the nightstand, half empty, with the remains in a plastic tumbler. The TV on the dresser, a gift from her grandmother, flickered softly in the dim room, emitting the low murmurings of a Sunday morning preacher, his voice rising and falling as he moved about a stage.

She was in a stupor, drifting in and out of consciousness, moaning softly at times. The cell phone, tucked between her arm and breast, buzzed and vibrated. She had no awareness of it. Not this time or the dozen other times in the last sixteen hours. Only the pain brought a degree of consciousness, and she sought the only relief she knew: taking two more pills and draining the last two fingers of rum in the tumbler. She lay still and prayed for it all to take effect.

The police officer stood on the stoop of the little white asbestos-sided bungalow. His fresh, clean face, close-cropped hair, and neat dress gave him an air of authority and professionalism that belied his youth. He noticed the volume of mail in the box, the uncut grass, and the dead flowers in pots on the porch before he knocked on the door for the first time. By the third time, he followed it with, "Anybody home? This is the police. I need you to come to the door."

With no response, he stepped off the stoop and walked down the driveway beside the house. He turned the corner into the backyard, almost tripping over an uncoiled garden hose left on the sidewalk. He repeated his knock on the backdoor with the same results.

A silver Toyota was under a cheap canopy at the back of the drive. It triggered a memory—something in the back of his mind, maybe something he had seen on this morning's daily report. He touched the radio attached to his upper sleeve. "This is Seymore 8. Didn't we have a report on a silver Toyota? I think it was a hit-and-run."

He walked to the car and waited for a response. As he circled the vehicle, he saw that the passenger front fender was crushed and a headlight was damaged.

"Yeah, we got something from last night – about 9:00 pm. A silver car, possibly a Toyota Corolla, left the scene on Farish Street. Left the road, took out a city bench in front of the Methodist Church, and hit one of those ornamental light poles. A witness only got a partial on the plate – last three digits 738."

"Alright – hold on dispatch." He walked to the back of the car. The last three digits were 138.

He sighed and looked back toward the house. "Dispatch, I may have the vehicle in question. I am at a residence on Hudson Street – not Hudson Avenue, but

Hudson Street. I'm here on a welfare check at the request of a family member. I believe we have cause to enter the residence, but I don't want to make that call myself. Send a supervisor out if you would."

"Got that Seymore 8. Should be there shortly."

CHAPTER 8

Sheriff Elam Thompson sprawled on a dark leather couch in his great room, his boots kicked to the floor, his big toe protruding from a hole in his sock like a topless turnip. He managed to doze between sips of imaginary tea and wet random kisses from the four-year-old playing on the rug. When he fell into a deeper slumber, his snores betrayed him and lent cause for the blonde-headed girl to bring him tea in a tiny plastic cup or whack his belly with her pink princess wand.

He had attended church that morning for the first time in weeks. He fielded questions about the murders that he couldn't answer and theories he couldn't politely dismiss from folks standing outside the little country church after services.

He ate his first home-cooked meal in a week at his mother-in-law's home: beef roast and potatoes, green beans and purple hull peas, cornbread, and the first tomatoes of the year.

He was full and sleepy, and content to lay there, regardless of his daughter's antics. He rolled to his side and fielded questions as he watched her stuff pink playdough into a teacup.

"Daddy, why do girls like pink and boys don't?"

"I don't know, darling, that's just one way boys and girls are different."

"Daddy, why does Sophie do that?" She pointed at the black terrier, vigorously scooting her backside across the corner of the rug.

"Her butt itches, and she doesn't have hands to scratch with. She probably has worms. We might need to get her some medicine."

"Eeww, do you put it in her butt?"

"No, it's usually liquid, and you put it on her food."

The cell phone in his shirt pocket danced and buzzed. He ignored it and closed his eyes. A few minutes later, it buzzed again. This time, he was too close to sleep to care, and he ignored it again, dreading what was coming next. The landline rang within moments. He waited and heard his wife talking with someone, obviously from his office. "He's right here; wait just a minute."

She handed him the phone. "It's Lindon."

In a tone that was too harsh, he said, "Yeah?"

"Boss, that Deeter woman called back late yesterday. She said her boy still hadn't come home. I talked to Dolan, and we went ahead and issued a BOLO to the city cops and the surrounding counties."

"You called me on a Sunday afternoon to tell me that?"

"Well, nawh. That's just it. We got a call just a few minutes ago. Wouldn't say who it was, but they were pretty upset. Said they saw a white truck that fit the description of Deeter's parked in with some junk vehicles behind that old, abandoned store out on Fielder Road - you know, where it intersects the highway. He said when he got close, he saw some blood on the door and got scared. Didn't want to get involved but thought we oughta know. I sent John Luke out that way. Just thought I should tell you."

Thompson sat up and ran his fingers through his mussed hair. "Yeah, you're right. Call me back on my cell when you know something."

He got up and went to the bathroom in the master bedroom, splashed water on his face, and ran a comb through his hair. He returned to the bedroom, sat on the bed, and began to change his socks. That damned hole had bothered him all day.

Caroline stood in the doorway, leaning against its frame. "You gotta go?"

"I don't know yet; maybe not. I'm just getting ready in case. It's been a crazy week—two killings in a couple of days. We didn't have but two murders all last year, and they were tied together. These don't appear to be. Now, maybe something else. They say bad news comes in threes."

She gave him a tired and apologetic smile and said, "Well, let me help you out with number three. We're overdrawn at the bank."

He leaned forward, his legs crossed and one sock halfway on. He didn't even question why. He knew why. He didn't make enough money. He thought of an expression that he'd heard from his grandfather. "Too poor to paint and too proud to whitewash."

He looked up at Caroline, who was now standing before him. "Tomorrow morning, go to the bank and pull a thousand out of the savings. That should carry us till I get paid next week."

She sat on the bed beside him and kissed him lightly before rubbing his shoulder with her left hand and placing the right on his knee.

"I think it's time for me to get a job, a part-time one anyway. She starts kindergarten this fall."

He nodded but didn't want to have the conversation. He was rescued when the cell phone danced again in his pocket. He pulled it out and said a little prayer.

CHAPTER 9

His boat would need a good cleaning, strewn with Styrofoam coffee cups, empty water bottles, dead minnows, and worm bedding. It reeked with the stench of bream spawn.

The fourteen-foot Alumacraft with a 25-horse outboard served his purposes well. Its small size and tough skin allowed easy access to water-bound forests of flooded stumps and cypress, and its shallow draw didn't spook the bream on beds in the narrow inlets along the shorelines of the watershed lakes that he fished when time allowed.

He watched the orange and white bobber ride the tender waves created by the steady breeze coming from the southwest. It had been a good two-day trip, a time to clear his head and slow his thoughts. But it was almost over. The sun indicated midafternoon, and the steadily increasing wind made positioning the boat more difficult than it was worth. It also signaled a coming weather change that would stop the fish from feeding.

Thirty more minutes and he would pack it in, head home, and have plenty of time to drop the fish off at Dwight's, who cleaned them on the halves. He would then wash out the boat, store it, and check the dozens of emails he was sure had accumulated in his absence before grabbing some supper with Mary.

As the fishing slowed, his thoughts turned to other things – as they always did. His fishing trips gave him time to ponder on things, life's bigger questions.

He had wondered all weekend if God ever laughed. Many years ago, he stopped questioning his existence and trying to attain some understanding of it all. His questions were more mercurial and curious now.

Does God laugh? His sense of humor was, without question, slathered in abundance atop all human interactions like whipped cream and chopped nuts. But does he giggle, guffaw, or roar occasionally with a good belly laugh? And if he does, is it the result of his own pranks upon his human herd or the absurd actions of humanity when left to its own devices?

He smiled at his mind's image of a white-robed, bearded God holding his belly like Santa Claus as he rolled across the floor of heaven in fits of mirth.

The thought was interrupted by the sound of a truck's horn. He swiveled his seat and looked across the lake to the boat landing. Sitting by the water's edge, next to a decrepit dock, was a white sheriff's department truck, its driver's side door ajar and only a ball cap visible above the window frame.

He gave a quick wave as he muttered to himself, pulled in his line, removed the bait, and attached the gold hook to the lowest eyelet on the limber fiberglass pole. He backed out into deeper water using the trolling motor, then kicked it out of the blue-green wash before returning to the back seat and pulling the starter rope on the outboard. It fired on the second pull, and he steered across the narrow lake, enjoying the wind and sun on his face as the old Alumacraft bounced over the dissipating wake of another boat that had passed a minute before.

Mac watched as the man walked away from the truck, leaving the door ajar and making his way onto the dock. It was a reserve officer, but he couldn't remember his name. He knew that meant that he was to be summoned for some purpose. If the Sheriff himself or his chief deputy had come, it might have meant a question or just a friendly visit, but this man's presence meant they were currently occupied with something significant.

He pulled to the dock, threw a yellow polyester rope to the man, and gingerly stepped out onto the half-rotten decking, his joints stiff, his balance suspect. He placed his hand on the deputy's shoulder for support. "Don't believe I know your name, son?"

The man was young and short. He hadn't totally filled out yet; his department's polo hung from his body.

"Josh—Josh Tuber, Sir. Sheriff Thompson said to find you and see if you could help him out. All hell broke loose this weekend."

"How'd you find me?" Mac stretched his back as he looked out over the lake.

"Your wife told us where you were. Just lucky you were fishing where I could see you."

"Well, what's he want?"

"Another murder. Dolan is tied up with the other case and he said he needs another pair of eyes on this one."

Mac knew about the shooting on Friday. "I thought that case was pretty well made - had the man in custody?"

The young officer looked momentarily confused. He removed his ball cap from his head and held it by his leg. "You been out here all weekend, I guess. This is the third one. We found a body this afternoon, too."

Mac didn't ask any further questions. He didn't want any more secondhand knowledge. He'd get the whole scoop from Thompson or Dolan. "Help me load the boat, then I gotta go by the cabin and get my gear."

He walked stiffly to his truck and backed the boat trailer down the landing while the young officer held the rope attached to the boat.

The boy just looked at him when asked if he could operate the outboard. "Alright, then you get behind the tailgate, latch the boat, reel it in and drive us out."

He climbed back into the boat, gave the motor a couple of tugs, and backed out into the lake for a straight shot onto the trailer. He made it on the first try and was shortly strapping the boat down before pulling the drain plug.

"Let me store my gear and get my stuff, and I'll be along. Did the Sheriff say where to meet him?"

"It's east of town, but he said just call him when you get back…… Catch anything?"

He reached into the boat and flipped the lid on an old, battered cooler. "Got about sixty bream – bluegills and a couple of catfish."

***

Bill "Mac" McKenzie was retired or semi-retired. Full retirement wasn't an option for most on a state pension. Some folks moved back to the home place and ran a few head of cattle, drove vehicles for local car dealerships, or, in the case of law enforcement, worked security at a casino or for ballgames at one of the state colleges.

Mac worked on an "as-needed basis" for the Sheriff's Departments in two small rural counties, serving as an investigator.

He was overqualified. Thirty-plus years in the business, first in a small police department in the Mississippi Delta, then in the City of Jackson, one year of insanity in New Orleans before returning to Jackson and finishing his career as the chief investigator of agricultural theft with the Mississippi Investigative Bureau.

Mary had finally had enough and put her foot down. She wanted to go home. She wanted uninterrupted family gatherings on holidays, a husband who slept in her bed at night, a vegetable garden, and some sense of normalcy before she got too old to appreciate it. He owed that to her, so they left the city and returned to their roots.

It was an easy transition for her. It had taken him a while, but eventually, weekly golf outings, fishing trips, and Sunday night church suppers worked their charms, and he was beginning to enjoy retirement, especially since he could still work on occasion.

It had taken less than an hour for him to grab his gear and make the fifteen-mile trip: first to his neighbor, Dwight, a tall black man of indeterminant age, who agreed to freeze his share of the fish for him, then home to unhook the boat trailer, change clothes, and leave a note on the kitchen counter for Mary, who was visiting her sister in town before she headed to choir practice.

He pulled out of the drive and made his way down the winding rural road, past small farmhouses and doublewides, modern steel hay and equipment sheds, and the few remaining ancient wooden barns decaying amongst the weeds that fed on the manure-laden soil surrounding the structures—soil made rich a generation ago by milk cows, brood cows, mules, and hogs.

His phone conversation with Thompson was short and to the point. "Don't come to the office – we're on the scene, eight miles east of Seymore at the intersection of Fielder Road and the state highway. Turn on Fielder, and we'll be behind the old store. I'll give you the details when you get here."

Mac turned southeast on a parallel road and circumvented the little town, cutting ten minutes off the drive. He hit the highway four miles from the scene and was soon on site. Two private vehicles were parked in the pocked asphalt parking lot at the front of the concrete block building, and a young deputy was leaning into the passenger-side window of one.

Once a busy country store, the white paint over the concrete blocks was almost gone—chipped, flaked, and faded. The windows were busted out years ago and were now covered with sheets of plywood. The gas pumps had been pulled, leaving a small raised concrete platform flanked by bollards on each end. There was no one else in sight until he pulled onto Fielder.

Three department vehicles lined the side of the road. A group of men stood near the closest. In the middle was Elam Thompson.

As Mac parked his truck, Elam walked toward him and motioned for him to roll down his window. He left the engine running. Thompson placed his forearms on the door frame and leaned in slightly. "I just wanted to talk to you without a crowd of folks around. I got a situation here, and I'm gonna need your help—maybe a lot of it."

"What's going on here?'

Thompson pointed toward the Ranger. "Looking through the window, it looks like shots to the head. I believe it's a kid named Jason Deeter, 23. Probably drug related. We haven't moved the body or searched the car- we were waiting on you."

"MIB crime lab on its way?"

"There ain't gonna be no crime lab – at least not today. They got a double homicide down in Jasper County, and it'd be six hours or more before they could get here. We've got rain coming in by dark, and I want to handle this before then. I just told them we'd take care of it. You up for it?"

"Guess I'll have to be. What's this I hear about another homicide?"

"Yeah, I got Dolan on that. We fished a car and a body out of a creek in the southwest part of the county yesterday."

"Sure, it wasn't an accident?"

"Yeah, unless he "accidentally" put two bullets in his head with a gun we can't find."

Mac switched off the engine, pulled a voice recorder from the glove box, and a small leather-bound notepad off the seat before opening the door and forcing Thompson to step back. "Well, let's get started. Are your guys taking photos, or do I need my camera?"

"Jimmy's got his – already taken a few of the location and the outside of the car."

Thompson waved Jimmy in, and they walked to the Ford Ranger. The ground was packed gravel mixed with patches of grass – no chance for tire prints. Mac made his first note on the pad. The truck was parked between two junked and picked-over cars: an old Impala on the driver's side and a rust-eaten Taurus on the other.

Mac looked at the closed driver's door. It was unlocked, and the window rolled up. The glass had marginal blood splatter on the inside, and there was a smear of blood above the door frame. The body inside could easily be seen, slumped across the seat.

"Photo," Mac said to the deputy. "Two straight on and one each at an angle from the front and back of the door."

After taking the photos, Mac leaned in for a closer look through the glass and turned on the recorder. After noting the location, time, and officers present, he began speaking as if to himself.

"Limited blood splatter on the inside of the driver's window near the top of the glass but some blood on the outside of the vehicle above the door, indicating that the victim was at least partially outside the vehicle with the door open. He probably fell or was pushed back inside after he was shot. The best estimate is that he was attempting to exit the vehicle when he was shot." He paused the recorder.

"It's probably not much use, but we should dust the handle, the glass, and the door edges for prints. Let's do the passenger handle first so I can get in and take a look."

He looked at Jimmy. "There's a kit in the back seat of my truck."

While the deputies began the dusting, Mac walked around the truck several times, searching for any telltale marks or additional blood splatter. On his second trip, he eyed the ground around the vehicle before stopping a few feet behind the deputies now working on the driver's side door handle.

After a moment, he said, "If this was an automatic and he didn't clean up after himself, there should be shell casings in the gravel near the rear tire or under the truck behind the tire."

In deference to Mac's age, Elam squatted down by the tire and ended up on his knees as he screened through the gravel with his now gloved hands and a ballpoint pen, returning almost immediately with two small brass casings. "I'll be damned – a twenty-two."

He placed them in a plastic evidence bag and handed them to Mac. "There's not much chance of a usable print on these as small as they are. Maybe the lab can get a partial."

Mac nodded but wasn't hopeful. "You guys through with the passenger door?"

Jimmy looked up from his work and said, "It's all yours – a couple of prints but mostly smudges – just what you would expect."

Mac and Elam went around the front of the vehicle and stood before the passenger door. Mac paused long enough to record the info on the shell casings. "OK, let's see what we got inside." They opened the door to the odor of dried blood and bowel release.

"Been here a couple of days."

Elam said, "Yep – been missing since Friday afternoon."

The body was rigid, the head suspended slightly over the passenger seat, the upper torso lay across the console. One leg extended into the driver's floorboard, and the other was scrunched onto the driver's seat and pressed against the door.

Mac took a breath of fresh air before leaning in and examining the head. There were two small round holes on the left side, one just above the ear and another in the neck just below and behind the ear. He lifted the head and found no point of exit. He made note of the wounds and the position of the body, and then, using Jimmy's camera, he began taking a series of photographs.

"I don't see a loose wallet or a cell phone, and I don't see any sign of struggle or other wounds. Looks like there's a magnetic holster attached under the steering wheel. Our next step is to get the body out and search it and the vehicle. You guys got a tarp and a body bag?"

After spreading a small blue tarp on the ground by the door, Mac supervised the removal of the body as they laid it on the plastic – rolling it over face down. Elam pulled the wallet from his right hip pocket and found the license.

"Yep, it's our boy, Jason Deeter." He dropped the wallet in an evidence bag and then began patting the front pockets down in case of a needle before searching them as well. There was only some loose change and a small cheap pocketknife—no cell phone.

Mac rolled the body over and avoided staring directly into the dull, dead eyes. He examined the face and neck for any marks or injuries and then examined the hands, finding nothing of interest. He also checked the arms and ankles for needle tracks, still finding nothing.

He rose and stood beside Elam. "I know I may be paranoid, but let's take his fingerprints here and not depend on the medical examiner to remember to do it. Besides, we will need them to eliminate them from any others we might lift."

They completed their task in a workman-like fashion and bagged the body, waiting for the coroner to sign off and then arranging for transport to the medical examiner's office in Jackson.

The search of the Ranger yielded the now empty magnetic holster on the steering column and a roach clip that had found its way under the driver's seat. There were no pipes, scales, or phones. A small bag of weed and an empty money clip were in the console. The key remained in the ignition, but the battery was dead.

By this time, Mac and Elam were seated in Mac's truck. Mac said, "Done about all we can do here."

Elam nodded. "We'll tow it out to the shop at the prison and have the crime lab come in when they can and give it a once-over. It doesn't look like there's much to work with, though."

"You know who called this in?"

"Nope. They called CrimeStoppers, so we ain't got a number to trace, but I got the impression it might be someone in the neighborhood who just saw something suspicious and got curious."

"What do we know about this kid?"

"Jason Deeter, 23. He was on parole. Served nine months of a two-year sentence for meth possession with intent to sell. He's been out about six months, and as far as we know - has been clean. He lived with his grandmother on the county side of Oakbind subdivision. She's been calling my office for two days looking for him. Not seen since Friday afternoon. The truck's registered to her."

"So, this probably happened on Friday night?"

"Yeah, I would say so. The body's pretty stiff, and the blood is completely dry."

"You said the other murder – two shots to the head, a young guy. – could be related."

"Hell, I hope so. I don't like the thought of two bloodthirsty bastards running around my county. Dolan has been working on it. How about we meet in my office at 8:30 in the morning, and we'll go over what we have? We should have some rundown on the fingerprints by then."

*****

Thompson's drive back to town was a slow one. He dreaded what he was about to do. Twice in two days was enough to mess with a man's head, even a jaded old head like his.

Like any parent, the old woman had obviously loved this kid and was hopeful of his future. He knew she would take it hard.

It was almost dark when he reached the small brick house on a residential street just south of town. Low rolling thunder could be heard in the distance as he stepped out of his truck. The wind had picked up, rattling the leaves of the large oak tree that stood near the corner of the house and blowing fast-food trash across the yard. The rain would be here within the hour.

He saw a curtain move in the front window, and as he approached the porch, a large, gray-headed woman opened the door and stepped out. Fear consumed her face. "He's dead, ain't he?"

He couldn't look her in the eye. He stood straight but his eyes examined his boots. "Yes, ma'am. I'm sorry to tell you that he is."

She wavered on the step – one hand raised to her mouth, the other searching frantically for something to give her support. She issued a low guttural moan as she melted into a mound of flesh and tumbled off the porch before he could reach her.

CHAPTER 10

The condo was dark except for the light emitted by the big-screen TV mounted on the wall. A movie from the 90's streaming from an online service provided background noise for his thoughts. He sat on a leather sofa in silk boxers and an expensive football jersey bearing the name and number of a University of Memphis college hero who had made it big in the NFL.

He felt strangely euphoric. The last few days had gone well, everything as planned except for the loss of the drugs, and if the cops found them – well, there was nothing that could tie those drugs to him. As always, he had covered his paper trail well, and at best, they could question him, maybe have some suspicion about overprescribing, but there was no proof of anything illegal.

The gun was a stroke of genius. He had already broken it down: clip, slide, and barrel, and then wiped each piece thoroughly three times with a soft rag before placing the parts in the paper sack at his feet. The remaining box of twenty-two ammunition lay in the bag as well. He repeated the process with Deeter's 9-millimeter and the two cell phones and placed them in separate bags.

There was one more thing to do. Rural traffic always slowed down after ten o'clock. Just a little trip. He had planned his route carefully – crossing over a series of creeks along two different roads—just a pleasant ride in the country on a rainy night.

He took another sip of Mexican beer from one of the frosted glasses he kept in his freezer. He realized that his actions meant his run here was just about over. It was time to move on – to some other little town, some other clinic, some other small struggling hospital desperate for a fellow with his qualifications. Maybe find someplace closer to Memphis – or New Orleans. New Orleans, where if you had money, you could get anything… and he had money.

***

When McKenzie pulled into his driveway, the sky was fading to black. What little light remained surged through the shades of purple and distant gray. Just enough light to illuminate the rain clouds rolling in from the southwest. The day had taken a fine course until his summons by the Sheriff.

He sat under the lean-to of the shop that marked the back corner of his property, looking across a wide expanse of fields and clumps of oak and hickory smattered with fast-growing pines. The warm glow of the lights from a private riding arena across the fence line provided a backdrop for a young female rider whirling and twisting her mount around a series of barrels, getting in those last rides before the red dirt and sand turned to mud.

He moved steadily in an old rocker with ragged rails, rails chewed by some pup, now long gone and merged into memory with a half dozen others. He had a habit of leaning to the side as he rocked, causing the chair to move sideways over time and forcing him to stop every few minutes and slide it back upon the concrete apron underneath the canopy.

The unusually cool June air, brought by the upcoming storm, and the distant light show behind the approaching clouds helped unwind the knots in his gut and the tension in his shoulders, allowing him to detach himself just enough from the afternoon's crime scene to take a broader view.

Forensics wouldn't be much help unless they got lucky with the fingerprints. It just wasn't that type of crime—no bodily fluids, no physical contact. This would be solved by someone who told somebody just a little too much, that someone telling someone else who just happened to need a "get out of jail free card" at the right time. When that happened, this case would unwind and fall neatly into place.

There was no question in his mind that Deeter's death was drug-related. They were all drug-related – even so-called crimes of passion, just like the murder of that girl a few days ago.

A missing cell phone also showed that he knew or at least had some contact with his killer. Why take the phone if there wasn't something on the cell to connect them? It would be easy enough to find the number, even if it was a throwaway. He'd take all the necessary steps tomorrow and have Deeter's phone records before the week was out.

The rain would be upon him within the hour. He hoped it would be slow and steady, providing a gentle rhythm that would ease him to sleep and provide a clean-washed morning.

He watched the dark outline of the deer playing near the edge of the first clump of trees, the old dog panting beside him, paying no mind to them as the light began to melt into the dominant darkness.

His thoughts ran from the case to chores that needed completion: cleaning the boat behind him under the lean-to, a batch of green beans that needed to be picked, a deck that needed to be washed, and a garage that needed to be swept. He rocked in silence, waiting to see the headlights of his wife's car as she pulled into the long driveway – the sign that it was time to go inside and finish the day.

CHAPTER 11

The coffee tasted like hell, coming from a pot that hadn't been cleaned in weeks, but it was hot and strong and black as coal. The briefing room was small and packed, and even at 8:30 a.m., the old HVAC system was struggling to cool a room with too many big warm bodies.

The rain during the night had cooled the air, but the heat and humidity had now returned with a vengeance. Summer had finally arrived and planned on sticking around for a while.

Thompson took the lead and provided a rundown on the status of each case. All three bodies were at the medical examiner's office in Jackson. Based on past experience, he expected preliminary results on Jason Dean by Wednesday and on Jason Deeter – maybe on Thursday. They would likely rush the autopsy on Deeter, considering the cases may be related. The woman's autopsy wouldn't be an issue. The final results wouldn't be available for weeks.

"Don't expect much – the only thing we may find out that we don't already know is if there were drugs in their system. The crime lab team arrived this morning and are going over Deeter's car as we speak. They've already processed the Altima. Again, don't expect much that we don't already know."

Mac broke in. "Anybody here doubt they are related – same shooter?"

Everyone nodded in agreement. There were too many coincidences: both young white males, both killed with two shots to the head, both had drug histories, and both likely killed with a small caliber weapon – and both missing cell phones.

Thompson looked at Dolan, who was reaching for his second doughnut from the cardboard box in the middle of the table. "Tell us what you got so far."

Dolan set the doughnut on a napkin on the table without taking a bite. "Not much. Jason Dean, white male, age 26, no adult record but was known to frequent a meth house out on Orangefield Road. We knew him, but probably only as a user. The only relative is an aunt, but she had little contact with him in the last couple of years. She did mention that she had seen him with a tall, skinny, redheaded kid - but no name. We got his cell phone number- at least the one she had - but it goes straight to voicemail." Dolan sat back in his chair and took a bite from the doughnut, a purple jelly oozing around the edges.

Thompson looked now at Mac but addressed the whole room. "I just brought Mac in yesterday on the Deeter case. Here's what we've got so far."

He flipped the page on a yellow legal pad. "Jason Deeter, age 23, white male on parole for meth possession with intent to sell. He had been out about six months and seemed to be keeping his nose clean – living with his grandmother. I haven't checked with his parole officer yet, and I don't have a cell number or known acquaintances. I'm working on a search warrant for the Deeter house and should have it later this morning." Thompson threw the legal pad onto the table.

"You guys are the investigators—you run your cases. Mac, I'm going to assign Jimmy here to do your leg work, and I'm going to work with Dolan. I don't have any deputies to spare. Jimmy, before you get started, work up a schedule and have Lindon bring in any reserves that are free to work to cover your normal workload."

Jimmy nodded. "I think I might know who the redheaded kid is—and where to find him. He may even be out on bond, so we could have some leverage with him."

"Good, maybe our first real lead. I got Lindon working on Deeter's cell. As soon as we find the carrier, we'll get a court order, get his call list, see which towers he was pinging off in the last few days, and maybe get some text messages."

Thompson stood up and pushed his chair back from the table. "I gotta have a smoke." He motioned for Mac and Dolan to follow him outside.

***

They each sat on a separate bench outside the courthouse entrance, forming a U shape. Dolan and Thompson were smoking, and Mac folded and unfolded a pocketknife in his right hand.

"Deeter's going to be a problem. I'm getting a search warrant this morning for the Grandma's house."

Mac's interest peaked. "Why? Granny won't cooperate?"

"Granny can't cooperate. She had a stroke last night when I gave her the news."

"Damn, That's rough. Is she gonna make it?"

"It doesn't look good. The ER doc said it was a massive one. Her prospects aren't good even if she survives. I haven't checked on her this morning. I thought maybe you could do that, Mac."

Mac nodded. Leaning forward, his hands clasped around the knife, he studied the feather line cracks in the concrete patio.

"This thing may bust wide open before the end of the day, but we sure don't have much to start with, do we? That whole Deeter scene just didn't feel right to me. You said you found a stash of prescription drugs in Dean's car. If it was a drug buddy – why didn't he take them? Surely, he would have known they were there somewhere, and why didn't we find any in Deeter's truck?"

"That bothered me, too. The way Deeter's body was in that truck – it didn't look like anybody took much time to search it. There was still a baggie of marijuana in the console. A low-level dealer would have taken that." said Thompson. "And Dean, I think maybe he didn't have time to search the trunk. It was in the middle of nowhere, but it was a public road. Probably didn't want to risk it."

Mac said, "I don't doubt Deeter was there to either buy or sell. If he was selling, he might have been smart enough to make sure he didn't have it on his person but close by. That search warrant's gonna be a while - I'm gonna run back out there and take a look around."

He looked at Thompson and smiled. "Right after I check on that old lady."

***

Mac's visit to the hospital was short. The duty nurse was not talkative; busy juggling patients and paperwork. He learned that Mrs. Deeter was alive, but there was little hope that she would ever recover. After promising an admissions clerk to inform the hospital if he found a next of kin, he headed east out of town.

He pulled behind the abandoned store, hoping to avoid drawing attention from the log truck drivers, farmers, and housewives traveling on the side road. He walked to the rear of the building along a short path worn through the weeds and junk that had accumulated over the years. A rusted and dented metal door stood slightly ajar, blocked by a clump of dead weeds and debris. There was no sign that it had been moved in months. He pushed lightly, but only the top half of the door gave slightly. He eased his shoulder into it, and it gave a foot or so- just enough for him to squeeze through.

The boarded windows across the front blocked any light, but the gaping hole in the roof provided more than needed. The floor underneath was covered with rotten decking and sheet roofing soaking in last night's rainwater, a line of water flowing toward a small hole in the floor that had once served as a cooler drain. The rest of the building was dry, its floor checkerboarded with ancient broken squares of tile that were popular in the 1960s.

The dust was undisturbed – no signs of footprints. The structure was empty except for a couple of wire racks toppled to the floor – racks designed to hold dime-sized bags of chips and cookies. There were no shelves, no counter, no coolers. No place to hide anything.

Mac backed out of the door and dusted off his shoulder before walking to the approximate location of the Ranger.

The kid had probably been dealing for a while, and he was on parole. He was probably smart enough to limit his risk as much as possible. If he were waiting on a buyer, he wouldn't want the merchandise in his possession but close by.

He turned to the old Impala, surrounded by foxtail and bindweed. The trunk was still latched, and there was no sign that anyone had recently walked to the front of the vehicle to open the hood. He tried the doors, and both passenger-side doors opened relatively easily.

The latch to the glovebox was broken, and its door flopped open – inside a couple of washers, an ancient auto fuse, and a paper clip. The front seat was no longer bolted to the floor, as if someone had tried to remove it and had been interrupted. He looked underneath the bench seat, in the rotted console, and even underneath the headrests. After searching the back seat, he was confident there was nothing there.

He turned his attention to the other wreck and then hesitated, looking back at the Impala. The remains of the car sat on half-size concrete blocks, and the tires and rims were long gone. He leaned down and ran his hand along the inside of the front tire well. Nothing. With some effort, he squatted and reached further. He felt plastic. He went to his knees and peered, his cheek against the fender. Two pint-size freezer bags were taped to the top of the wheel well with gray duct tape. He squared his body and with both hands, slowly removed the tape, pulling from the edges and set the baggies on the hood.

With an old man's groan, he straightened up to examine them. Oxycodone. Six pills in one bag, four in the other. Over the counter, Oxy costs about six dollars a pill. On the street, they could bring sixty.

He took photos with his phone, carefully placed the bags and tape in an evidence bag, and returned to his truck, where he scribbled notes onto his pad.

There had been prescription drugs in the other kid's car. The connection made some sense. Whoever killed these men was not a druggie looking to rob his dealer. If drugs were the purpose, the shooter would have waited until they were present before killing the men. The bullet wounds were too precise, the scenes too clean; nothing hurried or haphazard about them. This was planned. These guys must have been set up. The question was - why?

CHAPTER 12

The clinic had been busy all morning, as was usual for a Monday. Filled with mothers with kids in tow, coughing, wheezing, and eyes dulled by fever; young women and girls in shorts or yoga pants with sudden concern over their weekend activities; and middle-aged working-class men and women with aches and pains, high blood pressure, or diabetic symptoms: people who were too young for Medicare and didn't qualify for Medicaid. Hard-working men and women lost in the paperwork and high deductibles of government-subsidized healthcare.

Some were proud, determined to pay what they could, five dollars here or a twenty-dollar bill. But most came to the free clinic because it was just that - free. Hoping for a quick fix and a free sample pack of whatever medicine might ease their symptoms or cure their ills.

The converted wooden church sat on a corner that was the demarcation point between a once proud middle-class neighborhood that was determinedly fighting deterioration and one of two poor and highly segregated areas in the little town of Seymore: neighborhoods full of boarded-up HUD homes and housing projects.

The area to the east had once been a neighborhood of neat bungalows and ranches set amongst old oaks and hedges of azaleas and primroses, full of families and the drifting smells of six o'clock suppers, backyard barbeques, and fresh-cut grass.

It was now beginning to sag under the weight of a changing population and suburban sprawl. The occasional prim little home of an older couple or widow who refused to move was now the exception to rows of houses in need of repair and converted to rentals. Lawns went unmown and were full of bare spots. The azaleas crept to the edges of driveways and doorsteps before smothering under their own weight due to lack of care.

Streets and sidewalks, once filled on summer evenings with retirees walking their dogs and children on bicycles, were now void of activity except for the occasional gang of teenagers who laughed too loud and stared too long into open garage doors and sheds as they passed on their way to whatever mischief a kid could find in small-town Mississippi.

To the west, the two-story subsidized housing units melded with row after row of cookie-cutter, red brick single-family homes built in the sixties and seventies. Their carports spilled over with junk cars, cheap barbeque grills, children's yard toys, and plastic lawn chairs.

The white frame church's sanctuary served as a waiting room and admissions area. Its Sunday School classrooms used as examining rooms, supply storage and a small office where the minimal paperwork was completed. Its roof needed repair. Water spots dotted the ceilings. Due to its steep pitch and design, the eighteen thousand dollars required to reroof was the most significant item on a long wish list for the facility.

The waiting room was still packed at 11:30 a.m. Those with less severe issues would not be treated today; they would be sent home to wait until Thursday, when the doors would open again, or, if necessary, to the hospital's emergency room for service.

Lloyd Rich had seen twelve patients so far today. Actually, he had only seen eight. After a volunteer nurse took vitals and a description of their complaints, he prescribed light pain relievers or mild antibiotics without examining a few.

The other nurse practitioner was in the waiting room, a nurse tailing behind with a notepad, looking over the mass of patients for any that needed immediate care before closing the doors at noon.

Rich backed out of an exam room after a futile attempt to convince a large woman that she needed regular treatment for high blood pressure. He walked to the makeshift office to leave the last of his paperwork.

As he stepped through the door, he was greeted by two large feet up on the desk, feet clad in massive basketball shoes, feet attached to a pair of pipe cleaner legs crossed at the ankles. Leaning back in the old office chair, hands behind his mop of red hair, was Fugly Brown.

"Hi' ya Doc."

Rich flushed red. "What the hell are you doing here? I told you not to come back here for a while."

"Things change, Doc. We got to talk."

"You damn fool. Not here. Follow me. They'll be back here any minute."

He tossed his paperwork on the desk and waved for Fugly to follow him. He peered through the door, checked the hall, and then moved quickly to the last examining room nearest the back exit of the facility, pushing the skinny kid through the door before closing it behind them.

"Now, what the hell do you want?"

The man climbed onto the old examining table, its corners patched with black duct tape, and gave a gap-toothed smile. "I just wanna know what happened to Deeter and Dean. Thought you might could tell me." He peppered each sentence with a nervous, staccato laugh.

"What about them? What happened to them?"

Fugly studied Rich's face, then feigning surprise, said, "Why they're dead, Doc. Deader n hell."

Rich stood for a moment - silent, expressionless. He moved to the door. "You stay here. Don't leave this room. I'm going to be a few minutes, but whatever you do, be quiet and don't leave this room. If anybody comes in, tell them you have a backache." He aimed a stiff index finger at Fugly's chest.

Fugly smiled and lay back on the table, his hands once again behind his head.

It was almost twenty minutes before Rich returned. Fugly didn't rise but rolled over on his side, propping his birdlike head in his hand. His t-shirt rolled up over his stomach, and he began stroking the fine red hair around his belly button.

"Did you know I had a kid, Doc?"

"No."

"Yeah, me neither till about two weeks ago. Had to take a paternity test. I was pissed off at first, but he's a good-looking kid – just like his Daddy. I decided it was time to take some re-sponsibility." He stressed the first syllable of a word he had no concept of."

Rich was impatient. "What about Deeter and Dean? What happened to them?"

"Guess they pissed off the wrong fella, Doc." He grinned lopsidedly. "Shame about Deeter, him and me were good buddies. Sure would like to know who popped him."

He hesitated a moment, then sat up and tugged his shirt down over his white, freckled belly. "I know you weren't too happy with him."

"Deeter dealt drugs all over the place. From what I hear, so did Dean. Drug deal gone bad. Happens every day."

"Both of them?...nawh. Anyway, I know Deeter wasn't dealing meth or pot anymore. Said there was too much competition. A couple of Mexican dudes stepped in – flooded the market. Damned near giving that stuff away. A small-time dealer didn't have a chance to make any real money. Nope – all he was dealing was your pills, Doc. I hear that didn't sit too well with you."

Rich leaned against the counter, pushing back a glass container of cotton balls. "Deeter was stupid. I cut off his prescriptions a couple of weeks ago – end of story. He had a good thing going, a couple of hundred bucks a week, no risk. He got greedy, but I had no reason to kill him."

"That's not exactly the way I heard it. I heard he had you over a barrel, dealing your stuff instead of selling it back to you. He told me all about it. Hell, I even sold some for him. He laughed about it. He said he had flipped the deal on you, and you weren't too happy about it. Let's see—how did he put it…… He said you didn't like him shittin' in your nest."

"What do you want?" Rich was tired of the game.

"Well, Doc, I got a problem, and I know you can help me with it."

"I already told you I won't be writing you any more prescriptions. You're too careless, and you have a big mouth."

"Oh, I know, Doc, I know." He gave an exaggerated nod of his head. "It's just that I got responsibilities now – a kid to take care of. I got a sentencing date in a few weeks - second offense. They gonna send me up this time…eighteen months, maybe two years. I sure would like to know my kid and the baby momma had a little something to fall back on. I'm not greedy. Five grand would be enough. Otherwise, I might have to do whatever I can to get my sentence reduced. You know, like telling a story bout a local doc scamming prescriptions to poor folks, buying them back, and shipping them off to Memphis. I think they'd find that interesting. Not to mention that Deeter and Dean were a couple of them, poor folks."

Rich was stunned. "Where'd you get that from? Memphis, I mean, nobody ever said anything about Memphis."

Fugly just smiled and didn't answer.

Knowing he wouldn't get a response, Rich thought over his options. None of them were good. "I don't have five grand right now. It'll take a couple of days."

"Hell, Doc, I didn't expect you to whip it out right now. I'll come back here Thursday, although I bet a big-time medical man like you prolly got that much in your back pocket."

"I'm not a doctor; I don't make that kind of money."

"But you can sure write prescriptions, can't you, Doc?"

Rich ignored the comment and stood up, walking toward the door. "Don't come back here. It's too dangerous. I'll text you with a time and location when I get the money together."

"Nope. That's too dangerous for me. I don't wanna end up like Deeter or Dean. I'll be back here on Thursday – as a patient. I got this back problem, you know." He rose from the table, his feet smacking the old wooden floor.

"Oh, and Doc, just so you know, my baby momma's gonna be outside in the car waiting for me. We real close, I tell her everything."

CHAPTER 13

The search warrant for the Deeter home arrived at the same time that Mac returned from the crime scene at the abandoned store. Without returning to the courthouse, he met Jimmy in the drive of the small brick home—a typical cookie-cutter ranch of about twelve hundred square feet with three small bedrooms and a central bath, kitchen, living room, and utility behind the open carport.

"Don't happen to have a key, do you?"

"Sure do." Jimmy dangled a set of keys on a small purple fob. "Sheriff had to lock it up last night after the old woman stroked out."

As the deputy opened the storm door and searched for the proper key to fit the entry door, Mac reached into the black metal mailbox mounted beside the entrance and pulled out the mail - an electric bill, junk mail geared to the elderly, and a page of pizza coupons.

When Jimmy found the right key and turned the lock, all hell broke loose. The little lion of a dog stood stiff-legged by the corner of a couch, snarling, snapping, and yapping with the ferocity of a pit bull ten times its size. As the deputy stepped inside, the chihuahua raced forward and took a nip at a booted ankle before retreating to the safety of the side of the couch. The little dog trembled as he peered around the corner, continuing to growl and bark.

Jimmy cowered at the door. "Damn, that complicates things. Sheriff didn't say nothin' bout a dog."

Mac looked around Jimmy at the dog. "Ease on in. He's scared to death and probably hungry. Let me see what I can do with him."

Mac slowly moved into the room but at an angle away from the dog and headed into the kitchen. On the floor, near the sink, was a soup bowl half full of water and a small saucer that was obviously intended for food. He checked the counter and saw a two-quart glass container with what appeared to be dry kibble and a half dozen tiny tins of gourmet dog food.

"Let's feed him and see if that calms him a bit. He probably hasn't eaten since yesterday morning."

As he bent down to pick up the saucer, the dog ran forward as if to bite again, but Mac didn't react, and the pup scampered back to safety. Mac mixed a small serving of dry and canned food and placed it back on the floor. The chihuahua advanced and took a position under the small kitchen table, continuing to bark and growl.

"Now, let's go about our business and see if he calms down." Mac walked back into the living area and surveyed the room. Everything was as neat as a pin. There was no dust, and everything seemed to have a place. The dog continued to bark and growl softly.

"This ain't a meth house. This woman had some pride in the place. If we're going to find anything, it'll be in the boy's room or a garage or shed out back, I guarantee it."

They walked down the central hall and checked the first door on the right. It was clearly a spare bedroom. The bed was neatly made but covered in folded sheets, blankets, and an array of stacked shoeboxes. Bookshelves and small tables full of books, magazines, and knickknacks lined the walls of the room.

"We'll come back to this one."

The next door on the left led to a small but functional bath. The front bedroom at the rear of the hall was the woman's. The last room held a single bed, a flat-screen TV perched on a four-drawer dresser, and a couple of nightstands on each side of the bed.

"It's not going to take long to search this. I think I'll leave it to you, and I'm going to talk to the neighbors."

"Alright," said Jimmy as he slipped on a pair of latex gloves.

"Oh, and Jimmy, don't tear the hell out of the place. That old lady ain't done nothing to deserve that."

As Mac walked to the front door, he saw the dog eating from the saucer, pausing only long enough to growl and yap a few times before returning to his meal.

Through the storm door, he saw someone standing in the driveway looking toward the house. As he exited, the old woman frowned and stared him down as he advanced.

She couldn't have been more than five feet tall, leaning on a walker. Her thin but kinky hair, now a fine mix of black and grey, topped a coal-black face framed by round wire-rimmed glasses perched low upon her nose. She was dressed in a light house dress and cheap slippers.

"You the po-lice, I guess."

"Yes, Ma'am, Sheriff's office. Are you a neighbor?"

"Well, I ain't out fer a run." She nodded to her right at the house across a low hedge.

"You mind if I ask you a few questions?"

"You can ask, but I can't stand here all day." She motioned him to follow her as she crossed the concrete drive, picking up the walker with each step and slowly making her way through a break in the hedge.

He followed along dutifully, unsure what to do. "Can I help you?"

"Don't need no help, just gotta sit down." She inched her way to an ancient metal lawn chair beneath an oak by the corner of her home. As she sat down, she pointed to a similar chair.

My name's Bill McKenzie....and you are?

"Rose, Rose Nipples, but folks just call me Miz Sweet. Is she dead?"

Mac couldn't help himself and smiled. He imagined all the teasing and innuendos this woman must have faced over a lifetime. "No, ma'am. She's alive, but to be honest, it doesn't look too good. She had a stroke."

She stared across the yard, looking at nothing particular. "Always knew that boy would be the death o' her. That and the fact that she's fatter n hell. Eats crap all the time. House is always full of cookies and candy bars and them little snack cakes you buy by the box. She's a diabetic, you know, but she wouldn't listen to nobody."

"Are you good friends?"

She paused a moment, and her jaw seemed to tremble momentarily. "Yes sir, I guess we are; been neighbors for near twenty years. When you get older, friends get fewer and fewer, and you appreciate em more. You think it's strange an old black woman and an old white woman being good friends?"

"No, ma'am, not at all."

"When you get old, color of your skin don't seem to matter much."

"Yes, ma'am. How about the boy – know much about him?"

"Watched him grow up. Arlene's boy, that boy's daddy, he weren't no good. He got shot a few years ago trying to rob a liquor store over in Vicksburg. The boy's mom ran off when he was just a baby. Don't know what happened to her. Arlene never mentioned her. She raised the boy all his life. Did a good job, too, till he turned about sixteen. I know he's dead- heard somebody shot him."

"What happened when he was sixteen?"

"Same ol' thing. Runnin' around like a fool; dope. But it was strange. That boy doted on Arlene, always teasing her, lovin' on her, and helping her around the house. But then he'd go off and get into some kind of trouble, and she'd bail him out of it. She was always making excuses for him. It was like there were two sides to the boy."

"Yes, ma'am. Did he have any friends over at the house – anybody you could remember?"

"Not much. I seen a tall redheaded white boy a couple of times when he was workin' on that ol' truck of his….and one time when Arlene was out of town visiting her sister, I think he had a girl over—stayed the whole night. I didn't have the heart to tell her about it. Didn't figure it was any of my business."

"Do you remember what the girl looked like or know who she was?"

"No, it was after dark. All I could tell was that she was a skinny white girl. Ain't seen her since. That was bout two months ago."

She shifted the conversation. "Is Arlene in the hospital here in town?"

"She is. If she recovers, they may have to send her somewhere for therapy, though. She might not ever come home."

"She ain't got no family cept that boy and a crippled ol' sister in a nursing home somewhere near Vicksburg." Her voice trailed off, and she seemed lost in a deep sadness.

He watched her intently, searching for any sign of senility in her eyes and mannerisms. She seemed reasonably healthy and fully aware, except for the walker and a slight tremor in her left hand.

"If you don't mind my asking, Ms. Sweet, how old are you?"

"I'll be ninety-two next month. Done outlived my kid and two husbands. Too tired for another one…. Mr. Bill?" She looked at him over her glasses. "What happened to her dog?"

"The chihuahua? He's inside, yapping his head off. I guess he'll have to go to the city pound unless we can find somebody to keep him." He pulled his glasses down on his nose and looked back at her with the same mannerism, hoping for a response.

"Well, I don't want the damn thing – always barking and growling and pootin'. That's why she called him Toot. She fed him just like she fed herself: junk all the time. That dog's got the most god-awful farts you ever smelled."

87

"Yes, Ma'am – well, I guess we'll take care of him then. Can you think of anything else that we might want to know about the boy?"

"No sir, can't recollect anything I ain't already told you."

He reached into his shirt pocket and handed her a card as he rose from the chair. "Well, if you think of anything or if you need anything, just give me a call. You got anybody helping you? Do you need anything?"

"Sonny, I been taking care of myself for a long time. I get by. Just gotta find somebody to take me to the grocery store once a week. Arlene always did that, but I'll manage."

He walked slowly back toward the hedge, somewhat hesitant to leave her.

"Mr. Bill," She looked at him over the tops of her glasses again as she grasped the handles of her walker. "Bring that yappin' dog over here. The least I can do is take care of it till she gets home."

CHAPTER 14

Elam sat behind his desk, his boots on the floor beside him. A glass tumbler of crushed ice filled with a dark soft drink sat on the desktop, along with his service revolver and a series of plastic baggies.

"These two, I found out behind the store, taped in the wheel well of that old junk Impala. And these," Mac pointed at two bulging bags filled with soft yellowish pills, "were taped to the back of some drawers in Jason Deeter's room."

Mac took one bag and lifted it. "These are 15 milligram oxycodone. At $25 a pop, there's about $3000 worth here." Pointing to the second bag – "these are 30 milligrams. At $50 -$60, that's about $7500."

"Pretty good quantity for a small timer like Deeter. You didn't find any meth or weed?"

"Nope."

"Doesn't that seem strange to you? Does to me. Deeter went up on meth charges and a weapons charge. Most of these guys deal meth, and if they have pills, it's usually only a handful they get off a prescription or steal out of someone's medicine cabinet. Looks to me like he had a regular supplier."

Mac nodded in agreement. "I understand Dean had a big supply, too. It looks like that could be our connection. Do you reckon that supply is local or part of something bigger?"

"Hell, the supply may be local, but it's always something bigger." He paused and said, "I don't know, but these guys were two-bit. I can't see them involved in some big operation, but you never know."

Elam stood up and stretched, placing his hands on his lower back, and leaned backward. The black-framed clock on the wall said it was 5:05, which meant it was actually 6:05, as no one had bothered to acknowledge daylight savings time that spring.

"I need a good night's sleep. Haven't had one in months."

Mac looked at him closely and, for the first time, saw the wear in his face, eyes, and posture.

He empathized. "Yep, and it only gets worse as you get older when aches and pains set in. Just sleeping too long in one position will put a little fire in your hips or a cramp in your legs."

"Well, it ain't really that. Can't seem to calm my brain down." He had disclosed more than he intended and realized it immediately, but Mac's calm demeanor and maturity had put him at ease.

Mac thought back on his forties. The pressures of young children, financial uncertainties, efforts to make a name for oneself and build something that provided stability came to a convergence about that time in life. Throw in the near futility and sometimes horrors of law enforcement and the stress it brought; marriages and sleep were the first to suffer. His time in New Orleans had nearly cost him his wife and his sanity.

Mac looked out the window and said, "Somebody once said that sleepless nights are the result of our past and our present fears. Reminding us that our minds are full of traps, slips, and ghosts of the past."

He paused for a moment, grasping for a memory. "Filled with the backward march of dead pursuits and dying passions blocked by brutal beasts and collapsed dreams. The past comes alive on sleepless nights."

Elam looked at him and smiled. "That sounds like something out of a book. I didn't know you were a literary fellow."

Embarrassed, Mac sheepishly smiled. "I guess so, at least comparatively speaking."

To ease the awkwardness, Elam sat back down in his chair and slung his feet across the desk. "They're delivering me a couple of burgers- you want one?"

"No – thank you anyway. I got supper waiting on me at home."

"Good, cause I'm hungry – haven't eaten since that breakfast biscuit this morning."

Mac shook his head. "I'm getting too old to eat that way. I gotta watch my blood pressure and everything else. I'm just getting too old for all of this: bad hips, bad knees, bad feet. When I walk, I look like a short man riding a tall goat."

"I don't know, you look pretty good for a man of seventy."

"Maybe so, but I ain't but fifty-eight."

Elam grinned, creating doubt in Mac's mind about the seriousness of the comment.

Mac said, "I believe we got the Deeter boy's cell phone number from the old woman's phone bill. You got somebody to run it down tonight?"

"It'll have to wait until tomorrow. I got a shit load of cases to work – a half a dozen thefts around the county – four wheelers, trailers, even a damn farm tractor plus the usual stuff: domestics, assaults, and an old woman convinced that her ex-husband comes in her house every night and stands at the foot of her bed while she's sleeping. The only problem is, he's been dead for twenty years."

"Those are always fun."

"They're all fun till somebody shits and giggles. This one is probably early-stage Alzheimer's. And her son, her crazy-ass son, wants us to put a security camera in her bedroom and a deputy in the yard just in case."

The Sheriff scratched between his toes through his socks with the sharp end of a pencil. "The truth is most folks are a lot more upset about somebody stealing their stuff than they are about two dead drug dealers. I'm just glad the election is three years away."

Mac grasped the arms of his chair and leaned forward, readying himself to leave. "Maybe I can help you with those thefts when we get these solved. That's more in my line."

"That 'd be great 'cept I ain't got the money. At the rate things are going, I'll be $150,000 over budget by the end of the year."

"Maybe I'll do a freebie for you."

"Sounds promising. By the way – what's for supper?"

"Well, there were pork chops thawing in the sink this morning. If I know Mary, there'll be some fresh-sliced tomatoes, onion, cucumbers, and probably cornbread."

Elam shook his head. "You bastard."

***

Thompson had just taken the first bite of his second burger when Deitrich appeared in the doorway. Jesse Deitrich was short and stocky, well-groomed, and carried himself with a degree of arrogance. Approaching fifty, he was dressed in the standard outfit of an MIB agent: a blue dress shirt, khakis, cowboy boots, and a tan Stetson in his hand.

"How's it going, Sheriff?"

"Well, what do I owe the honor of your presence, Deitrich?"

"Just passing through on my way to Jasper County. Got a double homicide down there and a manhunt going on – all hands-on deck, kinda thing. Hear you got your own mess right here."

"That we do. Guess that means we can't expect any help from y'all anytime soon."

"Not much – not right now. I stopped by the prison and visited the crime lab boys. I brought all their evidence reports and left them with your dispatcher out here." Deitrich pointed outside the doorway. "Don't think they found anything you didn't already know. A few fingerprints that don't match the victims, but that's to be expected. They'll check those against MAFIS and send you the reports on those sometime tomorrow. Not much doubt that the murders are connected?"

"No doubt – think we found the connection but just don't know why."

Deitrich was silent – waiting expectantly, sure in his belief that a further explanation was obligated.

Thompson stared at the agent and then pointed at the baggies on his desk. "Opioids – prescription meds. Both were dealing – maybe exclusively."

Deitrich raised his eyebrows and leaned in for a closer look, taking the baggies and the half-eaten burger in his gaze. "Hmmph, that is a bit unusual in rural Mississippi."

The MIB agent stepped back and placed the Stetson on his head. "This is getting to be a big ol' problem in the populated areas—Jackson, the Coast, and up around Memphis. Check your pharmacies, your pill pushers, and your hospital—especially your hospital. You might want to check those prints with the Department of Health fingerprint unit. They got prints on all medical personnel in the state."

"Easier said than done with my authority down there in Jackson. Why the hospital?"

"Hospitals have their own pharmacies. Record keeping and controls are sometimes a bit lax. I guess you heard about the case over in Atlanta?"

"Can't say that I have."

" A couple of pharmacy techs were running a multi-million-dollar operation out of one of the medical centers over there. It went on for years, and they still haven't gone to trial. Plus, the easy money for your physicians is gone now. With all the cuts in Medicaid and Medicare and all the new regulations, it's hard for an honest doctor to make that Mercedes payment. The temptation is too great for some."

"Could be, but most of our docs are local boys. They drive pickups and Buicks."

Deitrich stepped halfway out the door and stopped. "Hope you're right. Look at your overdoses in the last few months. You'll find something in common with most of them. That'll be your man."

Diplomatically, Elam nodded. Anxious to get MIB out of his office, he said, "I'll do that, and I'll call you if I need a hand."

He picked up the now cold burger and took a bite.

Deitrich had to get in the last word before exiting. "Heard you had another shooting last week, too – Looks like Buford County is becoming the murder capital of Mississippi."

CHAPTER 15

The floor of the hospital corridors shone like glass, having just been waxed and buffed over the weekend. But the rest of the building showed its age. Outdated furniture filled the waiting areas and patient rooms, nurses' stations that hadn't been modernized since the 1970s, labs, X-rays, and an emergency room that had been retrofitted for more modern equipment—dangling cables and metal conduit filled with electrical wires in the middle of the room.

The cramped pharmacy near the center of the first floor of the two-story structure was home to Evan Winter, the only full-time pharmacist on staff. Evan worked eight to five, five days a week, while part-timers and contract pharmacists worked the weekends. A pharm tech came in each afternoon to inventory and assemble meds.

Loyd Rich sat in a cheap plastic chair in the corner of Winter's cramped office, sipping a soft drink. The buzz of a fluorescent light and the soft whir of the computer fan were magnified by the closeness of the room. He waited patiently for Winter to finish his last keystrokes to complete an order.

"We are going to have to cool it for a while," said Rich in a cold, toneless voice.

A look of fear crossed Winters' face. "Why? What's wrong?" He leaned forward, searching Rich's eyes from across the desk.

"Just being cautious. Couple of my errand boys got killed over the weekend. Nothing to do with us. Looks like they just got crossways with somebody. You know how these druggies are. But there will be an investigation, and they might find some of our stuff. They were stealing some off the top from us."

"Jesus, What the hell are we gonna do?" Winter's eyes got big, and he ran his hand across the back of his head.

"Nothing, exactly that – nothing. You kept the records the way I taught you, right?"

"Yeah, Lloyd, but still the volume of schedule two drugs I've been running through here" – Winters paused. "If they do an audit, there's going to be some questions."

"Let them ask their questions. If you did what I said, that's all it'll be - questions and doubts, but they can't prove nothing for sure. Besides, like you said, there hasn't been a thorough audit or inventory done here in years. It'll all be muddled up - it would take a forensic CPA to even know the right questions to ask, and there ain't a lot of them in this backwoods town."

Winter was silent. The pit in his stomach that he had since his first involvement with Rich had suddenly grown to the size of a basketball. "God, I wish I had never...."

His shoulders slumped, and he fell back into his chair. "Even if they can't prove anything, I could still lose my job, maybe even my license."

Rich stood up to leave. "Take a couple of days off next week. Make a long weekend of it and take your boys over to the Delta for some fishing – or maybe the coast. They say the speckled trout are biting off the marshes down there. Relax – keep your cool and go about your business. Probably nothing will come of it, and besides, pills are floating around everywhere – they can't prove they came from here."

Winters sat at his desk for a long time after Rich exited, wondering how the hell he got into such a damned mess. His hands trembled slightly as he opened his bottom drawer and extracted the small pill bottle he kept hidden inside a large box of paper clips.

CHAPTER 16

Mac never discussed his cases with Mary, a professional standard he had followed throughout his career. But he sometimes disclosed his encounters with the people involved. His experience with Rose Nipples was one of those encounters, one in which he made a point of sharing with his wife of thirty-five years. He knew what the result would be, and that was his intent. She said little, knowing full well what Mac expected of her.

"Sounds like a sweet lady. Where does she live?"

It was no surprise when he awoke the next morning to find his breakfast on the counter: a plate of biscuits, fried eggs, and country-cured ham covered with a tea towel and a half pot of coffee remaining.

Through the kitchen window, he could see Mary in the backyard garden. At this time of the morning, the air was crisp, and the sun was friendly, still content to provide a warm light without the heat that would later fry eggs on sidewalks, thus defining a summer day in Mississippi. She had donned rubber boots against the heavy dew, with old jeans tucked into the boots, and wrapped in one of his faded work shirts, now stained and frayed and usually relegated to a peg on the mud porch until needed for such a purpose.

Halfway down a recently tilled row, she was filling a grocery sack full of purple snap beans. At the end of the row, another smaller sack sat at the end of the row, full of tomatoes in various stages of ripeness.

Mac walked to the garden, a mug of coffee in his hand. "Guess you're headed over to Ms. Nipple's this morning?"

"Just thought I would take her a mess of beans. We've already put up more than we're going to eat this winter."

She smiled as she stripped a handful of pods dangling from the crisscrossed sawmill slats that formed a curvy backbone for the garden. She straightened and wiped a wisp of hair from her forehead with the back of her gloved hand. "Wanna help me?"

"Gee, Dear, I'd love to, but I gotta go to work. Besides, that's not the deal – I plant, and till you pick, we eat, remember?"

She turned back to her work. "Yeah, well, I never signed on to that deal. I guess that means you won't be home for lunch today?"

"I doubt it. Not sure where I'll be."

Without turning her head from her work, she said the phrase she had repeated thousands of times over the last thirty-five years. "Be careful out there."

***

The morning meeting had been short now that there were some specific leads to follow. Dolan took on the task of finding the carriers for the victims' cell phones, cajoling their records, and then cross-referencing any common calls between Dean and Deeter in the past few weeks or even months if necessary.

Jimmy Smith was running down a lead on the redheaded kid seen with Deeter.

Mac headed out to find the construction sites of two companies identified by old pay stubs found at the Deeter home. A quick trip to the local building supply yielded results.

The twenty-something clerk at the counter stepped away from the register as Mac flashed his badge. His yellow company vest was two sizes too small and clashed with the orange Stihl cap perched on his head.

"Cane Construction? Yeah, that's Jimmy Cane. They're building a couple of houses over in Tara Subdivision, but if you wanna talk to Jimmy—that's him over there." He pointed to a barrel-chested, freckled man of forty in a light straw hat signing purchase orders on the other side of the u-shaped counter.

The man looked up as he stuffed a pen into his shirt pocket and surveyed Mac carefully. "I'm Jimmy Cane. What can I do for you?"

Mac introduced himself as they walked outside and leaned against the hood of his truck. "I just wanted to ask you about one of your employees, Jason Deeter."

Cane scratched the side of his face and rubbed his chin. "I heard he got shot this weekend. Didn't seem to be a bad sort but I'm not sure what I can tell you. He only worked a couple of weeks, and that was" …. He paused for a moment… "back in April, more than two months ago."

"Why'd you let him go?"

"Well, I didn't really. He just quit showing up for work. He wasn't a trained carpenter – mostly clean up, and he was good with a hi-lift when we put decking on a roof. He was a fair worker and funny as hell – always cracking jokes. Pretty typical stuff. He worked well the first week, called in sick on Monday of the second week, and didn't show up at all by the third week except to get his paycheck. Said he just wasn't cut out for that kind of work."

"Did he have any friends on the crew, or did he have any problems with anybody?"

"No – most of my men are older, in their thirties and forties. They don't look for trouble."

"Did you ever see him hanging out with anybody? Maybe somebody picked him up from work?"

"I can't say that I did. We worked from 7:00 a.m. to 3:00 p.m., and he was always the first one out of there. At three o'clock, all you saw was his dust."

"Any sign of drug use?"

"No, I wouldn't tolerate that. The work's too dangerous. He was always a hyper kid, but that just seemed natural to him. I can't say he did anything that made me suspicious."

"Thank you, Mr. Cane. If you think of anything I might need to know, please give me a call." He passed a business card over, and Cane put it in his shirt pocket.

Cane shook his hand. "I hope you catch em —whoever did this. Like I said, he wasn't a bad kid."

By nine o'clock, he pulled into a developing subdivision where at least three new homes were under construction. He got a similar story from the other builder – a decent worker, not a troublemaker, and quit after a couple of weeks. This was going nowhere.

On his way back to the courthouse, he pulled into an old service station on the edge of downtown for a cup of coffee. The joe in the office was strong but tasted like hell.

The station had long ago been converted to a convenience store and deli, surviving on off-brand gas, beer, cigarette sales, and junk food sold at midnight to the potheads from the neighborhood. The place was empty except for the teenage clerk with a pierced lip and a splash of blue hair zipped across the top of her head.

"Good morning."

She acknowledged him with a nod and a curious stare, her elbows on the counter, her phone in front of her. He pumped a sixteen-ounce cup full of decaf before pouring powdered creamer from a canister and stirring with a plastic swizzle.

Bypassing the pastries on the racks and the breakfast tacos and biscuits in the food warmer, he pulled two bills from his pocket and handed them to the clerk. She was a pretty girl, except for the hair, the piercings, and the tattoos. Young enough to be his daughter, he thought. Who was he kidding? She was young enough to be his granddaughter.

As she pulled the change from the cash drawer, she dropped a coin on the counter. "Sorry, I just can't seem to hold on to the money today."

"Not a problem - that's a lifelong affliction for me." He smiled softly.

She was puzzled by the comment at first, but then a smile crossed her lips. "You're some kind of detective, ain't you?"

"I am – actually a Sheriff's investigator."

"I think my Momma goes to church with you and your wife – Mamie Temple."

"Sure- Mamie, she sings in the choir. I'm Bill McKenzie, but folks call me Mac. What's your name?"

"Tesha. Are you investigating the murders?"

"Couple of em- Dean's and Deeter's. Did you know either of them?"

"Knew em both – I liked Deeter. He was a sweet guy. Didn't care much for Dean though, even though he kept telling me he was my brother."

Mac put the change in his pocket, leaned against the counter, and took his first sip of coffee. "Your brother? I don't understand."

"I'm adopted. I don't know who my parents were. Jason kept saying that his Daddy was my Daddy, but I had no way of knowing that. He never would tell me how he knew either or say who he thought my Momma was. He was a weird guy. I think he was tellin' me this stuff to try to get me to hang out with him."

She leaned closer to Mac across the counter and lowered her voice. "I mean, why would you tell somebody they were your sister and then try to get into their pants?"

"That is pretty sick. How'd you know them?"

"They were always in here. Jason – Deeter, he was in here a couple of afternoons a week." She nodded toward the booths aligned against the wall underneath the plate glass window overlooking the gas pumps. "Dean, he would come in once in a while and sit with him. They'd go out back to smoke every fifteen minutes."

"Anybody else hang out with em?"

"Sometimes, Fugly would come around."

"Fugly?"

"Yeah, that's all I know him by. Use your imagination to figure out how he got that name. Skinny, redheaded guy always wears a ball cap. He looks like he belongs in the circus."

Mac realized that this sounded like the kid that Jimmy Smith was trying to track down. "Did you ever see them fight or argue? Did they ever do anything to make you suspicious?"

"I didn't pay much attention to them, Mr. Mac. I stayed away from them when Dean was around – he gave me the creeps. Once or twice, Delmer, the owner, would come out of the back and tell em to shut up when they got to laughin' or carryin' on too much."

"Did any of them ever try to sell you drugs?"

"Nope, they knew better. I may look wild, but I don't do that stuff."

"But you knew they were dealing?"

"Well, I didn't know – know, but it was pretty well known around here."

"I guess you see a lot coming through those doors. Hear a lot, too, I bet."

Mac took a sip of the coffee and eyed the shelf behind the counter, a shelf full of packs of small cigars, CBD supplements, bongs, and small glass pipes. He was saddened at the manner in which time had changed his small town.

"Do you sing, Tesha?"

"Around the house and in my car, why?"

"Come sing with your Mom in the choir sometime. You never know- you might like it."

Tesha scratched her arm and gave him a blank stare. "I ain't much for church, Mr. Mac. Besides, I work on Sundays."

CHAPTER 17

This would be his last package for a while. It included a simple note, typed and double-spaced: *"Hot here. Book sales may be slow for a while."*

Things had begun to unravel, nothing serious or even unexpected, but Fugly Brown was a complication he hadn't foreseen.

The normal method was safer and cleaner, but there wasn't time for that now. It had been a good system if everybody did what they were supposed to do, but now he wanted to get the drugs out of his possession and get paid. He would just let it play out and see what happened. With any luck, he'd be back in business in a few weeks. If not, there were other places.

He triple-bagged the pills and placed them inside an old thick medical dictionary, having cut out a cavity in the center of the book. He burned the remains of the pages in the gas fireplace of his condo. The book, also sealed in plastic, was then placed in a stiff cardboard box filled with packing peanuts, double-taped, and wrapped in brown paper cut from a supply of grocery bags bought at a Sam's Club months before.

The address label was printed on a cheap laser printer using common software. The return label carried no name, just an address of a common street and a non-existent house number. The postage was purchased online using a fake PayPal account provided to him. Mailed media mail. If all went well, in a few days, he would receive his payment in a package small enough to fit into a standard post office box that he kept under the name of a man he found on a tombstone in a rural cemetery. There was little risk of detection and the slightest risk of loss. He smiled as he thought of the simplicity of it all.

Supply was the only real problem in this business. Greed. He had gotten too greedy, doing business with a couple of kids that had shit for brains. Neither would have had the courage to cross him on their own, but together, they gave each other just enough nerve to test him.

They didn't concern him anymore. It was time to find a solution to his latest trouble – and Fugly Brown was trouble. He viewed the loss of the five grand as a cost of doing business. It was the next five grand and the next that concerned him.

He wondered if he should have kept the Ruger but immediately realized that would have been a mistake. He didn't need anything that could connect him, and that gun could send him to death row. He thought about Memphis – to ask for help but dismissed it at once. Too much to explain, too much to lose.

Doubt had begun to creep into his thoughts, and he wavered back and forth about his next steps. There was one thing he was sure of – it was time to prepare to move on. He had already begun his search for a hospital system in south Mississippi in need of a young, hard-working nurse practitioner.

*****

"John, how are ya?" he held the office phone to his ear, one leg stretched across his desk and the other crossed at the knee. He tapped and rolled a yellow wooden pencil across his ankle as he exchanged barbs with the Sheriff from two counties over.

"I need a favor."

A gravelly voice full of years of cigarette smoke and raw whiskey responded. 'Hell, boy, don't you know that's what I'm here for – to accommodate law enforcement in Buford County? Want me to drop everything and head on over there?"

"Would ya? We'll meet you at the county line with lights flashing – make a regular parade out of it."

"I bet you would, too. Alright, Elam, what can I do for you?"

"You still got that female deputy, the black gal?"

"Hell, son, we're uptown in these parts. I got three females in my department, two of em black. You gonna have to be more specific."

"Pretty gal, thirty-ish, a little heavy in the backside. I think she was at conference last year."

"That'd be Janie. Good officer. What do you want with her?"

"I need somebody that's not local – a little side work but nothing dangerous. It would just take a morning or an afternoon."

"Well, I suppose we could work something out…but why don't you have MIB send you someone? That's what they're there for."

"MIB's tied up down in Jasper County; besides, you know how slow they are. It'd take a week to process all their paperwork and get somebody down here. This is a simple little deal- all safe and cozy. She'll be home for supper."

"Well… I suppose we could work something out. I'm a little shorthanded around here. How bout we trade a few prisoner transports to your fine facility for her services? Like maybe two weeks' worth. That'd be about four trips."

"I'm a little shorthanded round here myself – what say we make it two trips?"

"What say we make it three, and you buy me dinner next time I come through?"

Elam smiled as he watched Mac walk into the office. "Sounds like a deal."

"I'll tell her to call you when she comes off her shift. What exactly do you need her to do?"

"Just a little visit to the doctor's office."

"There was a short pause on the other end of the line. "I see. A little fishin' trip, eh?"

***

Dolan had isolated the phones of the two dead men. As expected, they were burner phones using a prepaid carrier. The carriers were still researching the point of purchase but had been surprisingly helpful in providing call logs when they discovered the circumstances.

Deeter's list of calls for the last two months was sitting on the conference table, and Dean's was just coming in on the fax machine as Mac sat down, his fourth cup of coffee in his hand. Based upon his lack of success this morning, he was counting on the phone records.

Looking over the paperwork, Mac said, "Mostly text messages. I guess that's to be expected. We can track the numbers, but if I remember correctly, the messages are deleted after 4 or 5 days."

Dolan responded. "I've already asked. They're checking now. Might still have a few of Deeter's."

"Well, let's take a look." Working backward, they began comparing numbers. Deeter's last text was to a 505 number at 9:12 pm on Friday. Four texts that day to and from that number."

Dolan scanned Dean's call log. His last calls were made on the previous Wednesday afternoon.

"Let's see. The last call was at 5:15 p.m. to what looks like a generic carrier—two minutes long. Prior to that, there was a text exchange around 4:50 with a… well, look at that—a 505 number."

The numbers matched, but as they poured over the logs, the number never showed up again.

After thirty minutes and another pot of coffee, the records showed that the two contacted each other on a regular basis and had three numbers in common. One was the 505 number, another appeared to be a prepaid phone, and the third was to a common local carrier. Both logs showed an unusually high number of calls and texts from seemingly random numbers with various area codes.

"That seems odd, don't it?" said Dolan. "A couple of ol' country boys that ain't ever been nowhere but prison, getting calls from all over the country."

Mac nodded. "They're probably all coming from the same phone—some form of spoofing. We'll still try to run them down, though."

Dolan slowly shook his head in agreement, even though he wasn't sure he understood, and returned his attention to the printout in front of him.

As Dolan continued to scan the printouts, Mac rose and knocked on the Sheriff's door before entering.

"We're having some luck with the cell phones, but I've got a bit more to do before we have anything to report. I'm heading over to the hospital to check on Mrs. Deeter again, and I've got an appointment with the administrator out there. I'll see what I can find out about overdose rates and maybe ask a few questions about the pharmacy. Wanna ride with me, and I'll give you the rundown?"

"I can't—I've got court in a few minutes. Save it for the afternoon meeting. We made an arrest yesterday on a couple of our burglaries, and the guy's not local. I need to get his bond set as high as possible….and then I gotta run out to Sandbar Lake on a report of a vehicle in the water."

"Another one?"

"Pretty sure this one is an insurance deal – our stolen F150 from last week."

Elam looked across the desk at the investigator. "Mac, I don't like that hospital administrator- he's a little too pompous for me. He will probably try to stonewall you cause he thinks that's what he's supposed to do. Don't push too hard yet. Small-town hospitals are political as hell. If you see it's not going well, just back off, and I'll put some pressure on him from the hospital board. If that doesn't work, I'll call down to narcotics at MIB and get any overdose reports emailed up here. Just keep it generic for now."

Mac nodded without saying a word as he headed out of the office.

CHAPTER 18

Mac entered through the emergency room entrance. The waiting room was sparsely populated: a young mother with a child draped across her chest, a young man who looked like a construction worker holding his hand wrapped in a towel spotted with reddish brown stains, and an old black man slumped in a corner chair, head down as if asleep. He flashed his badge at the station nurse, and she waved him through the double doors.

He walked past the emergency bays, a small nurses' station, an x-ray room, and a series of doors labeled as offices and a doctor's lounge. He passed through another set of double doors at the end of the hall and entered the main hospital. The nurses' station for the floor lay beyond the pharmacy and a small waiting area. It took some time to find a nurse in charge who could or would tell him anything about Arlene Deeter.

"Not good, but better than we expected. She is awake but can't speak and is immobile."

The nurse was an older woman with gray hair, sharp features, thin and tough. She didn't look at him as she spoke but penciled notes onto a clipboard on the counter. "You boys had any luck finding a next of kin?"

"A little. But she doesn't have much. There's a sister in a nursing home somewhere around Vicksburg, but we haven't tracked her down yet. Probably won't be much help to you. You know her grandson was the boy killed a few days ago?"

"Yes, Mr. McKenzie, everybody knows that."

She paused and laid down her pencil, looking at him directly for the first time. "There are some decisions to be made: therapy, nursing home care, not to mention a power of attorney and all the legal stuff that has to be taken care of. I suppose we should contact DHS and get the ball rolling?"

"Yes, ma'am, I believe that would be the best thing to do. Can I see her?"

"I suppose you can, but like I said, she can't talk. Room 123, but you're going to have to wait your turn. She has visitors right now."

Mac gave a soft knock before slowly opening the door to room 123. Mary stood beside the bed, and Rose Nipples sat in a padded chair on the other side of Arlene Deeter, her walker perched beside her.

Mary smiled and half turned. "Ms. Sweet wanted to visit. Thought we'd stop by before we headed to the grocery store."

The old lady barely acknowledged him. She stroked Arlene's hand, leaning so far forward he feared she would tumble into the bed.

"Ms. Sweet has been so kind as to invite us for supper tonight. Six o'clock sound alright?"

"Better make it 6:30. Do I need to bring anything?"

"Just your own self...and don't be late."

***

Ed Lang's office was in the administrative wing near the hospital entrance, with a view of the emergency room just to the rear. The reception area was sterile and cold. The male secretary was behind a metal and glass computer desk. A small couch and two overstuffed chairs lined the walls, adorned with hotel-type artwork.

After a five-minute wait, Mac was ushered into the next office with a drastic difference in appearance. It was likely the only office in the hospital to have been remodeled in recent years. A large oak desk sat upon a plush dark blue carpet, the walls lined with dark wooden bookshelves and an assortment of western art.

Lang was a short barrel of a man with a ruddy face, thick neck, and hands. His dark suit appeared to be tailored and hung well from his body. He exuded self-importance.

"Officer McKenzie, what can I do for you?" He didn't rise as he motioned to a plush leather chair across from his desk.

"It's investigator, Mr. Lang. We're just trying to get some general information at this point. Overdoses that come through your emergency room – all those are reported to MIB- are they not?"

Lang frowned cautiously. "That's correct. We are required by law to report any verified overdoses to the state."

"Verified? What constitutes verified?"

He laced his fingers together and placed his hands on the desktop. "There are some individuals who accidentally overdose on their prescription meds – for example, cancer patients who exceed their dosage of painkillers – even early-stage Alzheimer's patients who forget they've already taken their meds. And then there are those who won't cooperate. By the time we run a tox screen, they're coming off whatever they took and just walk out. The law is a bit vague on the matter. We do the best we can."

Mac looked over his glasses at Lang. "So… if in the determination of the hospital, it's a case of accidental overdose or unclear, it's not reported?"

"Actually, it's the ER doctor's call. In those cases where a full tox screen wasn't completed or if that screen is inconclusive, it's up to the physician."

Mac shifted in his chair and crossed his hands. "How many doctors on staff work in the ER?"

"We have two ER doctors under contract, and when necessary, we supplement with a staff doctor or a nurse practitioner."

"And how many verified overdoses does the ER process in an average week?"

"Oh, I couldn't answer that without checking the paperwork, but I would guess three to four is typical."

Mac rose to leave and extended his hand across the desk. Lang took it but didn't rise. "Thank you for the information. We are pushed for time here. It may take a couple of days for MIB to get those records to us. Do you think it's possible for you to provide a set for our office?"

Lang frowned and hesitated. "Well, I don't know. I'm not sure what the legal requirements are for a matter such as this, but we certainly want to be of help."

"I'll have someone from MIB call you, or if necessary, we could get a court order. I do understand your situation."

Lang now made the effort to rise and slide from behind his desk, placing his hand on Mac's shoulder and almost imperceptibly pushing him toward the door.

"Of course. I can only assume this has to do with the killings that took place. As an employee, I hope Ms. Mayfair is not involved in any way."

Mac knew the problems that would follow if there was any uncertainty concerning the woman's status. Her job could be on the line.

"We don't normally discuss any details of an investigation, Mr. Lang, but in this case, I'll make an exception. No, we don't believe Denise Mayfair is involved in any way."

CHAPTER 19

Fugly Brown sat on the couch, flipping channels between a 70's cop show and some sad, silly reality program on MTV that somehow made him feel a little better about his life. "The baby was quietly sleeping in a carrier beside him.

He was a street-smart kid who seemed to attract trouble like an ol' bitch hound attracted strays. His Huck Finn appearance and attitude lent an air of coolness that generated an acceptance and near idolatry among the town's untethered and unmotivated teenage boys and young men. His wit and surprising verbal abilities made him the center of attention.

Tall and skinny, he almost appeared malnourished. His ever-present cap logoed with a capital A was worn and frayed, long ruined by grease and dirt slathered by unwashed fingers tugging at the bill. His pants hung precariously off his ass and seemed to contain nothing, although they sometimes billowed with the occasional escape of flatulent air. A mop of red hair flowed from beneath the cap and surrounded an acne-scarred face that was whitish gray. His skin was cratered and pockmarked, having the look of a recently plucked chicken wing.

Fugly was a low-end opportunist. Not a wise opportunist, but an opportunist, nonetheless. Selling drugs was not his goal in life. He knew it was a dead end. But he felt it was the only path left to him at the time, given his aversion to honest labor or education, and now he was going to pay the price for it.

He looked at the girl in exactly the same way. She had been an opportunity, and he had taken it, and now he was paying a price for it, too.

Hell, he didn't know what to do with a kid, and he had no desire to pay for that kid. But she was stubborn. She was going to have her money, and in some way, it made him respect her. At some level, he felt a desire to do the right thing by her.

Work had never held any appeal for him. Hell, he didn't know how to work. He had even tried it a couple of times: first, a job at a chicken factory and then hauling shingles for roofing. Damn, that was hard. And it required him to follow a schedule. Something he could not comprehend. Rising early every morning, being at the same place at the same time. It was too much to ask of any man.

A knock at the apartment's door in the subsidized complex on the west side of town forced him to rise from the sofa for the first time since noon. Fugly looked through the peephole and recognized the clean-cut man outside as a cop. He cursed under his breath before taking a deep breath and opening the door.

"Hi' ya, Fugly."

Fugly shaded his eyes from the afternoon sun at the deputy's back. "Do I know you?"

"Yeah, Buford County Sheriff's Office. Need to talk to you."

Fugly opened the door further and walked back into the room as he asked, "Somethin' wrong? Not a problem with my bond, is it?"

Jimmy Smith smiled and said, "Not yet. You were buddies with Dean and Deeter, weren't you?"

"Oh, so that's what it's about." He sat back on the couch, lit a cigarette, and took a deep drag before blowing the smoke out of his nostrils. "Yeah, I knew em – weren't bosom buddies or nothing, but I knew em – small town, you know."

"I'm gonna need you to come down to the courthouse and talk to the Sheriff. He has a few questions for you."

"When?"

"Right now, would be good."

Fugly shook his head and pointed at the child. "Keepin' my kid till his Mom gets home from work. Maybe tomorrow."

"What time does she get off work?"

"Five o'clock, I think. Hell, I don't know. Sometimes, they make her stay longer if somebody from the night crew doesn't show up."

"After five is fine. He'll be there. Just buzz in, and he'll open the door."

Fugly fingered his cap and said, "Well, I'll try. My car's in the shop. Don't have the money to pay my bill. If'n I can catch a ride, I'll be there."

Jimmy's manner changed. "Just be there. I'll even come to pick you up and bring you back." He handed him a card with his cell phone number.

Fugly leaned forward and took it, searching for another excuse but thought better of it. "Alright, I'll call you when she gets here. Don't know that there's much I can help you with. Terrible thing, though. Deeter was a good guy. I can't believe what happened to him. And Dean - heard he drowned?"

Jimmy wasn't sure how he should react, but as he walked back to the door and grabbed the knob, he turned and gave a hard look back at Fugly. "That's what you heard, huh?"

Fugly's smug composure broke slightly as he averted his eyes from the deputy, and all he could do was nod.

As Jimmy walked back to his truck, he pondered on the lie. Everybody in town knew that Dean had been shot- so why the lie? Maybe a guy like Fugly just couldn't help but lie to a cop.

***

When Jimmy returned to the courthouse, he found Thompson, Dolan, and Mac in the conference room, stacks of phone records scattered about the table.

Dolan was frustrated. He didn't like paperwork and had risen to stretch. He stood in a corner leaning against the counter that held the coffeemaker, a box of junk food, and an honor jar full of change.

"Damned confusing, I can't make heads nor tails out of all this."

Mac didn't look up as he leaned back in his chair. "We've just got to stop and think like these guys would.

Let's assume that Deeter and Dean were killed by their source. They did something that pissed them off or something that could expose them. We know they all had burner phones – Just found out that Deeter and Dean bought theirs locally. Hell, Deeter even used his own name to register the phone. But the source, he's gonna be more careful. That's why all the different numbers and the calls without caller ID."

Dolan looked confused. "There ain't no way he could have that many cell phones."

"Nope – probably just one phone with a proxy service or a masking app."

Dolan's expression indicated that further explanation was needed.

"It's easy to block your number. Your phone has that capability, but of course, when someone dials your number, it's stored in their call log. It's significant that the guy didn't block the 505 number. We got it coming in and going out like he never used it before and didn't intend to use it again."

Mac leaned forward and adjusted his glasses. "All the other calls are coming from one phone using a masking or spoofing app or a paid proxy service that generates a new number each time you make a call."

Thompson looked at Dolan and said, "It's similar to all those spam calls you get for car warranties, security systems, and health insurance that seem to come from local numbers."

Dolan dumped two sugar packets into a Styrofoam cup and then sat down at the conference table. "So, all we really got is that 505 number."

Mac frowned and pushed the glasses up on his head. "Which means we probably got nothing. I'll bet you that box of doughnuts - that phone was bought in a convenience store three states away and is now at the bottom of some creek in the next county over. We can track down where the phone was purchased and even get an email address needed when it was activated, but the email won't tie back to anyone."

Dolan scratched his cheek and then hung his arm over the top of his head, tugging at his ear. "So, what do we do?"

Mac looked at Thompson for approval. "It's a long shot, but we can find where it was purchased. If it was recent enough, we might even have surveillance video, or somebody might even remember the guy."

Thompson hesitated for only a moment. He was tired and still had a long night ahead of him. "Yeah – might as well. Got nothing to lose but time and money."

"Once we get any more phone records, there are other possibilities," said Mac. "We can track the cell phone towers that it pings off of – get some kind of pattern. If we had a suspect, it could get interesting."

Dolan looked doubtful. "How's that gonna help us? We still can't tie a suspect to the phone."

Mac smiled and rose from his chair. "Maybe no – maybe yes. Our guy is gonna have his personal phone as well. It would be suspicious if he didn't have one and if people didn't have his cell number. If we knew who he was, we could also track the personal phone and compare the times and locations with the burner."

Thompson nodded. "If we only had a suspect. Let's start tracking down that burner phone in the morning. He looked at Mac with some envy. "Guess you're going home to supper now?"

"Nope. Got a dinner date with two lovely ladies, but I can stick around for a bit."

Jimmy spoke for the first time. "Boss, that Brown kid is supposed to be here after five, but I got a feeling he's gonna have some excuse not to show."

"Well, go get him. Tell him I'll pull his bond if he ain't here by six. I ain't got the patience for this shit. I'm going into my office, taking my boots off, and calling the wife. Don't bother me till you bring him in."

***

Jimmy returned to the complex just in time to see Fugly exit the ground-floor apartment. He stuck his hand out the cruiser's window and waved him over. At first, he thought he might run, but he saw the man's shoulders slump before he ambled over to the deputy.

"Get in the back seat. When the Sheriff gets through with you, I'll take you anywhere you wanna go."

As Fugly crawled into the cruiser, he said, "I just wanna warn you, I got some bad gas. The girl brought some chili home from that fast food place she works at, and it's been workin' on me."

"Uh huh, I'll roll the windows down, but try to control yourself. I damn near live in this car."

Fugly smiled and raised himself slightly in the seat as an acrid odor filled the cab. He sat back with a satisfied sigh.

Jimmy's reaction was immediate. "Damn, boy! You're gonna have to clean your drawers after that one. We're only five minutes from the courthouse – don't do that again."

"Sorry, but Mom told me to never hold my stinkers – said it was bad for your health."

"You do that again, and I'll be bad for your health."

A few minutes later, Fugly stood in the doorway of Thompson's office, flanked by Jimmy. Mac sat in a rolling office chair in the corner.

"Sheriff, this is Alan S. Brown. Most folks know him as Fugly. He's just been dying to talk to you."

"I bet." Thompson waved him to a hardback chair across from his desk. "Where'd you get the nickname?"

"I don't know – grade school, I guess. Only politicians get to pick their own nicknames. It don't bother me, though. Kinda like it now- sorta rolls off your tongue, don't it?" Fugly looked at Mac but did not acknowledge him.

Elam didn't respond as he looked through a file in his hands. "Alan Sylvester Brown, second conviction, sale of meth, driving on a suspended license, and possession of a handgun by a convicted felon. You've been a busy boy. You got a job?"

"In between right now. It's a small town, and everybody knows your business. Plus, my sentencing is in a few weeks. Nobody gonna hire me knowing I'm going away for a while."

Elam nodded. He leaned back in his chair and swung his stocking feet up on the desk, one big toe protruding from another hole in the sock.

Fugly focused on the toe and said, "All that stuff that paper says I did – that's over with. I'm a family man now. Got a kid to help take care of."

"Hope so, Fugly, hope so. How are you supporting yourself?"

"I ain't really; I'm living with the baby momma. She pays the bills. I mow a couple of yards for a man once in a while for some pocket money. That's about it."

Elam tossed the file on the desk and crossed his hands across his chest. "I need to talk to you about Dean and Deeter. It's pretty ugly the way they died. Thought you might know something that could help us."

Fugly sat up straighter in the chair and looked directly at Thompson but kept his focus on the bulb of a toe. "Don't know what that would be. I knew both of them but ain't been hanging around them much since I got straight. Deeter was a pretty good guy, always joking and carrying on, lived with his grandma. Dean- well, he was alright., at least most of the time."

"What do you mean – most of the time?"

"He kinda had a mean streak sometimes. Always pushed people too far. He was bad to animals sometimes, too."

"For example?"

"Well, if he saw a dog on the side of the road, he'd speed up or swerve just to try and hit it. Damned near wrecked us once. A couple of years back, at a party, I saw him throw a kitten off a second-floor balcony. Stuff like that."

"Sounds like a hell of a guy."

"Don't get me wrong. Most of the time, he was okay; it's just that sometimes he'd get in one of those moods—dark, you know."

"Mostly when he was using?"

"Yeah, I guess so. But like I said, I ain't been hanging with those guys lately."

Elam asked, "What was he using?"

Fugly seemed surprised by the question. "Hell, I don't know – weed, meth – whatever he could get his hands on. I never used that stuff – maybe a little weed, but I wasn't into all that."

"You just sold it, huh?"

Fugly broke a slight smile. "Ain't no point denying what you already know."

Elam's tone changed slightly, and he focused intently on Fugly's face before he asked, "You ever seen either one of them with pills, you know, prescription stuff?"

Fugly looked down at his hands and hesitated as if he were searching for the correct answer. "Can't say that I did, but like I said, I ain't been around all that for a while."

Elam smiled slightly and asked, "Do you want a cup of coffee or a soft drink?"

"A Coke sure would be good right now – maybe settle my stomach."

Elam pressed the intercom button on his desk phone and asked Lindon for two coffees and a Coke. He sat silently as they waited. The silence was uncomfortable for Fugly. He crossed and uncrossed his legs and rubbed the dry skin on his elbow.

When Lindon delivered the drinks, Elam saw Jimmy through the open door, exiting the entrance with two cans of air freshener in his hands. He wondered what all that was about.

"Either one of them have a girlfriend?"

"Naw, never saw Dean with a girl. Deeter had one for a while. She was hooked on meth. Her family got her and sent her to some treatment place. I ain't seen her since. That was a few months ago."

"How bout where they hung out?"

"Sheriff, I don't know. I done told you, I ain't around that stuff no more!"

Elam's manner changed again. A hard expression cemented to his face as he pulled his legs from the desktop and leaned forward in his chair. "I'm going to give it to you straight. Both those boys were dealing. I can prove it. You've been seen in their company within the last few months. I got enough right now to pull your bond, and you can sit in my jail until you're sentenced. But….," he drew the word out to make his point, "if you give me something useful, I can ignore that. If you're real useful, I might even speak to the judge and get your time cut down, but so far, you ain't been much help."

Elam paused. "Maybe they stole from somebody, maybe they were just too careless, but whoever was supplying them killed them – neat little bullets to the side of the head. I wanna know who that is."

Fugly's cool shell began to break. "I swear I don't know who it is." He paused and tried to gather himself. "There's a house out on Orangefield Road. I think Dean stayed there sometimes."

"That would be the old Camfield place?"

"Yeah, Otis Camfield and his little brother. But I don't think there was any serious dealing goin' on. Them boys use too much to run something like that. It's just a party house- people go there to crash and get high."

Elam knew the property well. Rebecca Camfield died a few years back and left the old farmhouse to her two boys. She had spoiled them after her husband's death, and neither one had held a serious job in their life. The oldest was probably pushing forty.

The place on Orangefield was a regular stop for his deputies – fights, ambulance calls for overdoses. But the boys were smart enough to sweep the place before his deputies arrived. He could recall at least two cases where overdose victims were found on the front porch. The brothers claimed they just showed up on their doorstep.

"That ain't much, Fugly. I already know about that place, and you're right; those two ain't got the guts or the sense to do something like this."

Fugly was nervous now. Spending the next few weeks in jail would screw up his plans, but revealing too much would screw them up even more.

He shifted his weight in the chair and said, "A few months back, Deeter did tell me he had a deal going on. He showed me a baggie with some pills- I don't know what they were, but he said he was making good pocket money. I know he wasn't making any big money. He wanted to know if I wanted in, but I was already in trouble and didn't want no more. I swear that's all I know."

"He didn't tell you where he got those pills?"

"I swear to God, he didn't, and I didn't ask. If it would help me any, I could ask around, but I don't want to get into any more trouble."

Elam stood up and placed his hands on his desk. 'Why don't you do that, Fugly. It might be worth your time – that and if you happen to remember something you forgot to tell me. Jimmy will take you wherever you need to go. Give him your cell number; you better come a runnin' if I call. Got that?"

"Yes, sir." Fugly got up and walked to the door. "I need to go to the store – need some baby formula."

CHAPTER 20

The young woman lay on her back in the stiff hospital bed. An older lady, concern and frustration exposing her age, sat in a nearby chair as the police officer stood at the foot of the bed, a pad and pen in his hand.

"Well, you look better than the last time I saw you. Hope you're all right."

The girl didn't respond but stared blankly at her mother. She twitched slightly and looked as if she wanted to pull the covers over her head. Her eyes lost their first hardness, and she looked to her mother for escape, for her to somehow make it all better, to make it go away, to make the cop and the questions go away.

The young officer sat in a chair beside the bed, signifying that he wasn't leaving until he finished his business. "You've got some damage to city property you're gonna have to pay for. Since it's obvious that you were impaired and you left the scene, your insurance company probably won't cover it. This is gonna be on you."

He held out a slip of paper. When she ignored it, he handed it to the older woman. "You'll be on the docket of city court next week. You'll get a letter about the specifics.

If you're still in the hospital at the time, call the court clerk, and she'll work it out. It'll all be in the letter."

The young woman in the bed didn't respond but simply looked to her mother.

"We understand, officer. We'll take care of it." The older woman answered with a defeated tone.

He nodded before he continued. "Now, there's a matter of the narcotics we found in your house. Oxycodone, I believe they were. Did you have a prescription for those - 'cause we couldn't find one?"

The young woman panicked, flexing her body hard against the bed and pounding her head against the pillow. "Momma, I think I'm gonna be sick. I gotta get in the bathroom!" She threw back the sheet and raced toward the door of the bath, slamming it behind her.

Her mother leaned forward in her chair, wringing her hands. She looked at him with pleading eyes. "Officer, can we do this later? I don't think she's up to it now."

The young man shook his head. "She's got a possible possession charge hanging over her. If she answers some questions and gets help, that might go away."

The woman spoke to her hands in her lap. "She's not a bad kid. She got an injury playing soccer when she was a senior in high school, and she got hooked on painkillers. The damned doctor was dispensing pills like it was candy. We've been fighting this for three years. She got out of treatment six months ago, and we sent her here. We have family here and figured a small town would be better than Jackson. I guess that wasn't such a good decision."

The officer responded flatly. "Yes, ma'am, I understand, but she can help herself with the legal issues if she talks to me. Does she have anything on her record?"

The woman hesitated and then nodded. "She's got two possession charges and a DUI." She looked at the cars in the parking lot just outside the window, obviously reliving some bad memories. She acted as if she wanted to say more, to make excuses, but she just couldn't bring herself to do it.

He nodded again before tucking his pen into his shirt pocket. "Well, you need to know that another charge will likely lead to forced treatment, and if she refuses that, she could serve some time. If she would give us some information that might lead to getting some of these drugs off the street and goes to a treatment facility on her own, I believe the judge will offer a deferred adjudication and keep this one off her record."

She paused, took a deep breath, and sought to explain herself. "Chrissy's our only child. All we know to do is try everything. Last year, we tapped out my 401K and borrowed money from my husband's parents to get her into treatment. Right now, he's trying to get her into a facility on the Coast but it looks like it will take a second mortgage this time."

She rose from the chair, stiffened her back and determination shaded the face that had just moments before expressed nothing but shame and sadness. "Do you have any children, officer?"

"No, Ma'am."

"When you do, you'll understand. You'll do anything for your child – I mean any damn thing."

She sat back down, her elbow now on the arm of the chair, and held her chin in her hand. "Let me talk to her. Her head's just not straight. I'm afraid she would hurt herself if she thought she might actually go to jail. I will get her to talk to you; just give me a few hours."

The officer rose from the chair, obviously thinking over the options. "Someone will be back in the morning. Probably a county investigator. I think they might have an interest in this." As he walked to the door, he turned and said, "She's the only one that can help herself now. Good luck to you, ma'am."

***

"That's some fine fried chicken, Ms. Sweet."

"Well, there's more over here, Mr. Mac. Help yourself."

He waved his hands in surrender. "Couldn't eat another bite."

Mary poured coffee from an old-fashioned percolator into three mismatched cups, one advertising a local cotton gin that had been out of business for nearly thirty years; the others were obviously dime store purchases from many years ago.

"Come have a seat, Ms. Sweet. We'll clean up later."

The older lady turned from the sink and was about to object until she saw the smile on Mary's face. She pulled a saucer from the cabinet, moved her walker from beside a chair, and took a seat across from Mac.

She'd had a habit, a seventy-five-year habit of cleaning her kitchen immediately after a meal and rarely broke it. It showed. Her kitchen was spotless, almost shining, in spite of the fact that everything in it was at least fifty years old. The cabinets were original to the house, a house built in the late 1940s in the housing boom spurred by returning servicemen and their families. It was well-built but thrown up quickly and simply. The chairs and the metal table with the Formica top were 50's kitsch. There was no dishwasher. The only concession to modernity was a small microwave on the counter.

Mac lifted his cup and before taking a sip, asked, "How's the dog? Toots, wasn't it?"

"Doin what he always does; fartin' and barkin'. I got him locked in the bedroom right now."

She spooned the coffee into the saucer, held it to her lips, and blew across it. Looking over her glasses, first at Mac and then at his wife, she asked point-blank, "What are you folks doing here?"

Mac shared a smile with Mary. Suspicion between the races was always just below the surface, especially among the older generations.

"Just being neighborly, ma'am. Mary wanted to meet you and help you get groceries, and I had a feeling you were a fine cook. Wasn't wrong either."

Sweet looked him in the eye, searching for a sincerity she seemed to find. "You know, I ain't had guests for supper in more than twenty years. Last time was when my second husband died … and before that, when my boy passed."

"Tell us about them."

She stared into the cup at the black pool before responding. "Not much to tell. Roy, that was my boy; he died of cancer when he was fifty-five, never married or had kids, so I got no grandbabies. Virgil was a few years older than me, passed in his sleep. Just didn't get up one morning."

Mac said, "Virgil Nipples? Don't believe I remember him."

"No, sir. His name was Turner. When he died, I took back the name of my first husband. Virgil was a good enough fellow, but our marriage was what folks nowadays call… what is it—a marriage of convenience. He had a good pension but no home. I had a home but not much money coming in. It worked out good. I got fond memories of him."

Mac continued. "And your first husband, was he a good man?" The question brought a curious stare from Mary.

Sweet was silent for a moment, and he feared that he had crossed a line in their blossoming friendship. She looked across the table, adjusted her glasses, and responded:

"How a man's remembered by other folks ain't always got much to do with what he done. The world'll take care of that. If folks liked him, then they'll hold him up to the light and let him shine. If'n they didn't, they'll just forget him or make him a devil until the world changes again and flip-flops him into another thing he never was. He was good to me. I guess that's all that matters."

The silence was uncomfortable until Mary broke it with a question she rarely asked. Still, she was grasping for something to change the subject. "How's the investigations going?"

Mac looked at her with surprise. He hesitated and spoke slowly, deliberately. "It's a tough one, but we've got a few leads."

Sweet seemed to wake from her memories. She spooned more of the coffee into the saucer. Before lifting it to her mouth, she said, "That boy weren't nothin' but trouble for Arlene, nothin' but a heartache. I guess he never had much of a chance, though. She spoiled him like most grandmas do."

"Yes, ma'am."

The words seemed to spill out of her now. Lacking someone to talk to for so long, they flowed like water over a dam.

"There's so much for them to get into these days. Back in my day, there weren't nothing but rotgut whiskey. That was bad enough. I don't know, maybe it was worse."

"Yes, ma'am, I remember those days, but you're right. There's a lot more trouble these days."

"Seems the parents bout as bad as the young'uns. Seems like we just livin' to sin. God told us that from the beginning. People always lookin for another way to sin. Nowadays, we just can't face all those fine ideas and thoughts of the folks before us – folks who learned lessons from them hard times and with the salt to deal with em. You know what's wrong, don't you? Too many gadgets. All of them smart folks comin' up with gadgets to free our time so's we can sin a little bit more."

"Yes, ma'am. I believe you might be right about that." Mac drained his cup.

Mary sought to change the flow of conversation again. "Let's finish the rest of this pot. Mac and I'll wash the dishes and let you get to bed. It's getting late."

Sweet broke into a smile and laughed, more of a cackle.

Mary was amused but puzzled. "What's so funny?"

Sweet clapped her hands and said, "I never thought I'd see the day. White folks in my kitchen, washing my dishes." Her eyes twinkled with mischief.

As they walked to Mac's truck, he grabbed Mary's hand and held it like a young lover. "Never thought I'd meet a genuine philosopher tonight."
"Yep, she's quite a lady. Sharp as a tack. I like her."
"I thought you would."

CHAPTER 21

    Mac stopped his truck at the end of his long driveway and stepped out to pick up a paper carton full of chicken bones and soiled napkins tossed beside his mailbox. The trash along county roads was an ever-increasing problem since the state no longer allowed prisoners to walk the ditches picking up cans, bottles, and fast-food wrappers. Officials claimed it was an insurance issue, but Mac knew there were underlying political reasons for the stoppage.

    He was always befuddled that in an area as beautiful as this place he called home, full of people who hunted, fished, farmed the land, managed their timber, and took great pride in their manicured landscapes, some chose to scatter their leavings along rural highways and country roads.

    Unfortunately, dump piles blossomed across the more isolated areas, where people who didn't want to be bothered with the twenty-dollar fee or make an effort to visit the county landfill, raked out construction debris from the beds of trucks or dumped old furniture and appliances in road ditches and dead-end turnouts.

    He tossed the greasy box into a plastic trash bag he kept in the back floorboard and turned to survey the freshly mown hay in the neighbor's field across the road. The grass had been laid down two days before, and the sweet, dusty aroma was still present. As the morning dew began to rise during the morning, the dark green cuttings would take on a soft gray color. A late morning fluffing would be followed by a mechanical rake creating windrows that snaked across the field.

This was a second cutting; good hay with high protein content used for horses, square baled, and sold from the field. Local horse owners would begin arriving by late afternoon with trailers and teenage boys, anxious to show their feats of strength by tossing the bales to a stacker perched six to eight feet atop an ever-growing pile.

The smells of hay, tractor exhaust, and human sweat evoked strong memories of his childhood, a time when thousands of bales were stored in lofts and hay barns to feed his father's herd of black Angus through the winter. Summer afternoons where he worked shirtless, soaked in sweat that captured the dust and hay residue - clinging to his skin, leaving dirt rings around his neck and an angry rash and abrasions on his arms and belly. Work only stopped when the evening dew moistened the bales. Then, he and his brothers would take a flying leap into the farm pond on the edge of the field, washing off the worst of the dirt and hay. He smiled at the memory and headed into town.

The morning's meeting was slow to develop. Dolan was still working on cell phone information and had managed to find the carrier for the 505 number, but a purchase location would take some time. Fugly Brown had only confirmed information that was already suspected. The Camfield brothers' property was undoubtedly a drug den, but there was no evidence of a tie-in to prescription drugs or the deaths of Dean and Deeter. With limited resources, further investigation in that direction was on hold, at least for now.

By 8:30, Thompson had received a pair of phone calls that jump-started the morning. A message from Ed Lang authorizing his department to review hospital overdose records for the last three months was followed by a call from Seymore PD concerning a young woman, Chrissy Triste, who was hospitalized from overuse of prescription drugs and alcohol. He scribbled the particulars onto a pad on his desk and passed the note to Mac as he entered the conference room.

"Guess I know what I'll be doing the rest of the morning." Mac looked at the note before folding it and tucking it inside his shirt pocket.

"He said that the girl is pretty fragile – scared to death of jail time. If you handle her right, she might be useful."

"Use my fatherly appeal, eh."

"Whatever it takes."

Thompson returned to his office to face a stack of incident reports on his desk. Over his shoulder, he said, "When you pick up the report, get a list of nurse practitioners and pharmacists as well. It's time we started looking at some of them."

"That reminds me." Mac pulled a note from his pocket and handed it to Thompson." I got some license numbers yesterday when I was out at the hospital. There were a couple of F-150s in the employee's parking lot. I kept thinking about that gray one you mentioned in the Dean case. One of those is a charcoal gray King Ranch. I thought it might be worth checking into."

The Sheriff nodded and closed his door, tossing the note on top of the pile of papers documenting ATV thefts, domestic abuse, and drug arrests. He remembered the license plate numbers he had gathered days before and had forgotten to follow up.

***

The wiry old nurse manned the nurse's station again. She barely looked at him when she directed him to Chrissy Triste's room, just two doors from Arlene Deeter's. Still focused on her paperwork, she pulled a pen from behind her ear and stated, "By the way, she's awake."

"The Triste girl?"

"No," she said. "Mrs. Deeter. She can move her left arm a little and mumble, but she ain't ever getting out of bed again. Just thought you'd like to know."

"Thank you. I'll check in on her." Feeling dismissed, he walked down the corridor and knocked on the door to room 125.

He found a young woman in pajama pants and a t-shirt sitting in a chair beside the bed. An older lady shuffled through hospital paperwork while sitting on the foot of the bed using the overbed table as a desk.

Chrissy Triste looked freshly showered, her hair still wet. He quickly realized she displayed the physical symptoms of opioid withdrawal. She held a tissue in her hand and was continually wiping her nose. She constantly shifted position in her chair, and her face was flushed. She averted her glance after her first eye contact.

The older woman reached over the bed and turned off the television that was playing low in the background. She pushed the table back and rose to greet him, standing beside the edge of the bed.

"Ms. Triste, my name is Bill McKenzie. Folks call me Mac. I'm an investigator with the Buford County Sheriff's Office."

The young woman merely nodded as her mother stretched her hand toward him. "I'm Jane Triste, Chrissy's mother. She's doing a little better today."

Mac took her hand and squeezed slightly. She met his eyes with a face mixed with gratitude, hope, and fierceness. It had been years since he had dealt with drug cases, but it was an expression that he remembered well.

Some young people had no advocate, just parents who had long ago given up on their children to maintain their sanity or who just weren't equipped to deal with all the turmoil and sorrow that addiction brought to their family. But there were others blessed with parents, a spouse, or a sibling who devoted everything, their financial stability, their energies, and their hearts to finding a path out for their addict. Chrissy Triste was obviously blessed with the latter.

He turned back to the young woman. "Seems you have a bit of trouble. Maybe we can help each other. Are you willing to do that?"

She never looked up as she brought the tissue across her nose but slowly nodded.

"Good. How long have you been using?"

"She was in treatment until a year ago. She got…"

Mac held up his hand and stopped the mother. "Let her tell me."

He looked at Jane Triste with a knowing smile. "Maybe it would be better if you waited outside. Maybe you could bring Chrissy a soft drink and some ice while we talk. Sometimes, it's easier to talk freely without a family member present."

Jane started to protest and then realized he was right. She had been here before. "I'll be outside in the waiting room."

When her mother exited the room, Chrissy turned her head toward the window. "I started again about six months ago. I was clean for a while, but – I don't know." She started to cry softly.

Mac pulled another tissue from the box on the bed and handed it to her. She took it without looking at him and sat silently, dabbing at her eyes and nose.

Mac had seen a lifetime of addiction. Addicts who hated themselves for the havoc they were wreaking on their bodies, their minds, and their loved ones. Others who were so far gone, so entrenched in the life that they were incapable of remorse or guilt, only living day to day, fix to fix. He believed that their brain chemistry changed, that the drugs took over like a demon of biblical times, focused only on destruction. At times, he hated them all for their weakness and selfishness, but then waves of sympathy fostered by his Christian background and the example set by his wife would all but overcome him. Neither emotion was conducive to his work in law enforcement.

"You don't know what?"

"I don't know why I started again. I just did – ok!"

Mac sat on the small hard couch beside the girl in the chair. "Addiction's a hard thing. I've seen a lot of it in my job. I'm not here to preach to you or shame you. I can't help you with that- that's all on you. But maybe I can help you with the legal stuff that's about to come down on you. Tell me where you got the pills."

She swallowed hard and grasped the arms of her chair, trying to calm herself. "I got the first ones from a doctor."

"You mean a doctor here- in Seymore?"

"Yeah, Doctor Barton. I went to him about my leg, and he gave me a week's prescription. When I went back, he wouldn't give me any more. I think he got suspicious and said he would need my medical records from my last doctor before he would write another one. I knew I couldn't do that."

"So, what did you do then?"

"I got them mostly from Jason.

"This Jason – do you know his last name?"

She shook her head. "I didn't ask, and he didn't tell. You know how it is."

"Can you describe him for me—his age, hair color, size? What kind of car did he drive?"

"He was about my age, maybe a little older. He had brown hair and was a regular size. He wasn't fat or muscular, if that's what you mean, just kind of regular. He drove a red or maroon car, maybe a Toyota or a Nissan. It wasn't really old, but it wasn't new either."

"And where did you meet him at – to buy?"

"After a while, he would come by my house every few days, but if I ran out, I'd go look for him. Usually, I found him at a house out on Orangefield Road or that old convenience store on the edge of town."

"Do you know if he had other pills besides just Oxycodone? Was he the only one you bought from?"

She eased her grip on the chair and grabbed another tissue. "Oh yeah, he had a lot of stuff – Valium, Adderall, other stuff I didn't know. I used Valium, too. He was the main one I bought from, but sometimes, there would be another guy in the car when he came to my house. He never got out of the car, so I don't know what he looked like, but sometimes Jason would go back out and get what I needed from him."

"Chrissy," He reached over and touched her hand. "This is important. Did you have or possess any illegal prescriptions?"

She looked at him for the first time, caution in her eyes. "What do you mean?"

"I mean, did a health care professional write you a prescription that you weren't supposed to have or offer to buy the pills back from you after you had it filled? Or did maybe, Jason give you a written prescription in exchange for some of the pills?"

She paused, her eyes returning to her lap, searching for her words carefully. He'd seen it before—a suspect trying to find the right words that wouldn't be incriminating.

"Mr. Mac. I never did that, but one time. Just a few days ago. Jason had been trying to get me to take prescriptions around to all the pharmacies. Been asking me for months. He said I could keep some of them, but he never said how many. I wouldn't do it because he wouldn't let me unless...." She hesitated, never looking up. "Unless I had sex with him, of course, he didn't put it that way. I wouldn't do that – he was a creepy guy." She again began to cry softly. "But I did take that one."

There was a slight tap at the door, and her mother entered the room, a canned soft drink in her hand. She looked at Chrissy and saw the tears. "Do I need to go back outside?"

Mac nodded. "We're almost through. If you hang around outside, I'll come to talk to you in just a minute."

The woman backed out of the door, the soft drink still in her hand.

"Do you know where he got the prescriptions?"

"No, sir." She looked at him while drying her tears. "Mr. Mac, I want you to know I never slept with him."

"That's good to know, Chrissy." He patted her hand again and rose. "Good luck to you. I hope you get straightened out. I just want you to know you have some good parents. Lots of folks aren't so lucky."

"Yes, sir, I know." The tears began to flow again.

"By the way, where did you get that prescription filled, and what was it for?"

Mac exited the room to find Jane Triste standing outside the door. He led her to a small waiting area and sat beside her.

"They're dismissing her before noon. We've got her in a treatment facility a couple of hours from here. Are we going to be able to take her today?" She looked at him plaintively as she spoke.

He paused, considering his options. "I'm not supposed to do this. I'll have to square it with Seymore PD. It's their jurisdiction, but I think we can get the possession charge dropped since she's voluntarily going into treatment. There are a couple of things you need to do now."

He reached for a pad and began scribbling. "And by now, I mean before you leave town. Here are the names of a couple of local attorneys. Get one of them to represent her. They can handle the court stuff and prevent any more legal trouble."

He passed the pad to her. "Write down your contact info in case I need to talk to her. Probably won't, but we may need to interview her again."

She shook her head as she wrote on the pad. "I don't know what to say but thank you."

CHAPTER 22

"So, did you turn up anything?"

Elam leaned into the window of the small hatchback. He had made the pre-arranged traffic stop on the west edge of town, and the young black woman handed him her license to legitimize their meeting to anyone who might be watching.

"Nothing that you can use. He seemed clean to me. Didn't even blink when I asked about diet pills. He said I didn't need them and he wouldn't prescribe them, and then he handed me a low-carb diet pamphlet. I don't think he's your man, or he's really cautious."

"Well, it was a long shot anyway. Just been hearing some rumors and thought I'd better check it out." He handed the license back without even looking at it.

The woman tossed her hair and placed the license back in her wallet. "I got a free physical out of it. Found out my cholesterol is high and headed toward diabetes. Too much pork and cheese grits, I guess." She looked at him intently through the window. "It was free, wasn't it?"

Elam smiled and placed his hands on the door. "Yeah, of course. Just send me the bill at the office but mark it

ATTENTION with my name. This is unofficial. I don't want to start rumors or damage someone's reputation."

"No need." She said as she reached into the passenger seat and handed him an invoice with a long list of lab tests.

He whistled when he saw the amount of the charges.

"I couldn't give him my insurance, so I had to pay upfront. He was actually a pretty good doc; seemed a little preoccupied though."

"Maybe so. Etau is not a local fellow. He came here a couple of years ago and opened his clinic. He serves mostly the black community, and people like to talk, especially bout folks who are a little different. I never put much stock in it, but I wanted to check it out."

The woman started to speak but then hesitated before cranking her engine. "You don't need a female deputy, do you?"

"I always need a good one, but I don't have any money to hire right now. I'm over budget, and these murder investigations are gonna put us in a hole till the end of the year."

He looked at her, trying to discern her level of interest. "You're not happy over there with Sheriff John?"

"It's alright, but there's not much room for advancement. I'd like to be an investigator one day." She looked out the front windshield, her hands on the steering wheel. "Is that what this is all about—those killings?"

Elam smiled and stepped back from the vehicle. "Send me your particulars. I'll keep them on file. You'll be the first one I call when something opens up."

She nodded and shifted the car into gear. "I'll do that." She paused. "There was one thing. I didn't think much of it at the time. The clerk who took my money, after she looked over my paperwork, leaned in and almost whispered to me that next time, I ought to try the free clinic over on Brand Street. Said they had some good nurse practitioners over there. Now that I think about it – it seemed kinda strange." She pulled into a line of traffic and left Elam standing on the side of the road.

***

Mac and Elam arrived back at the courthouse at almost the same time. Mac handed the overdose list and the list of employees requested to the Sheriff as they walked into the back door of the office.

"Might have something, but it may take a subpoena. That girl was getting her pills from Dean. The way she described him- there wasn't much doubt, and in the last few days, he gave her a prescription to fill."

"Is that so."

"It was filled at Jergen's on the square. Wanna walk over there with me?"

Elam looked at the stack of paperwork on his desk and hesitated. Then he smiled. "Why not? I need some fresh air anyway."

Jergen's Pharmacy was only a half block from the courthouse's front door in an old downtown row building flanked by the Magnolia Diner and a woman's clothing store that seemed to change names and owner's every few months.

The walk around the square took longer than expected when Elam was stopped by a local attorney who insisted on a discussion about a client who had recently been arrested on domestic abuse charges. He eventually extricated himself when he promised a meeting in his office later that afternoon.

As they entered the doors of the pharmacy, they were greeted by a burst of cool air – almost cold. The pharmacist station was in the rear of the retail area, behind rows of cold medicines, headache remedies, and greeting cards. The station was manned by an older lady and a young woman wrapped in a sweater in the process of writing a customer's name and particulars in an old-fashioned ledger book.

"Thank you, ma'am. Be sure to take these with meals, or they'll upset your stomach. Ruth will check you out."

The young woman with red hair and freckles turned to them with a level of curiosity in her eyes. "May I help you?"

Thompson broke into his politician's smile. "Is Doc Jones around?"

"Yes, sir, he's in the back. Would you like to speak with him?" She continued writing her entries into the ledger.

"Yes, Ma'am. Privately, if we may."

She eyed the two men closely. "You law enforcement?"

Thompson held her gaze and said, "Just tell him it's Sheriff Thompson."

***

Elam and Mac were ushered behind the counter into a small, cluttered office where Doc Jones poured over paperwork. Spectacled and graying, Jones was a small man full of nervous energy. He had built a fine reputation in the little community, serving on city boards, church boards and heading charity events. He had acquired the handle, Doc, because, in earlier and simpler days, the poorer folks in town preferred a visit to his pharmacy rather than local doctors. When he could, he would provide over-the-counter remedies, bandages, and antiseptics to those who refused other medical treatments.

All the men knew each other, and their greetings were cordial.

"Well, Elam, what can I do for you?"

"Doc, I can't say too much yet, and I'll ask that you keep this between us for now, but we're investigating the deaths of those two young men last week. We believe there may be a drug angle to all of it."

Jones stiffened and grabbed a pen from his desk. "I see." He waited for more information.

"Let me assure you, we're not suspicious of you or your pharmacy. Let me make that clear right now. However, we are interested in a prescription for oxycodone that was filled here last week or the week before. We think it might be a forgery."

Jones was silent for a moment as he placed the nub of the pen in his mouth. "Well, Elam, you know I'll help in any way I can, but you do understand I can't just let you go through my files. I could lose my license, not to mention any lawsuits that might arise. HIPPA, you know."

"I know, Doc. Just giving you a heads-up. We'll be getting a warrant. What's your policy on keeping paper prescriptions?"

"We're required by law to log every prescription. We handwrite them and record them in a computer file at the end of the day. As far as the actual paper the prescription is written on, we're required to keep those for only five days."

"Damn, this might be more than five days ago. I'd really like to see the actual paper and signature."

"It's not a problem. It's our policy to burn them, and we keep them until we get a box full before I take them home and burn them in my trash barrel. There's probably six months' worth back there."

Thompson and McKenzie looked at each other and smiled. "That's great—it might be the break we need. We'll have a warrant either late today or in the morning. We appreciate your help."

Jones seemed relieved. "Not a problem. If you tell me what you're looking for, maybe I can save you some digging through the paperwork."

Thompson thought momentarily and was about to consent when Mac caught his eye. "It's best that I don't say anything. No need for you to be more involved than necessary. Tell us about the process when it comes to written prescriptions."

Jones leaned forward, placing his elbows on the desk, and interlaced his fingers as if he were lecturing. "Not much to tell. We don't handle too many written prescriptions anymore. Most come by computer, and a few are even still faxed to us from the doctors' offices. Written prescriptions come from a pad created by the doctor with a watermark and the physician's particulars. We're careful with those. Are you sure it was filled here?"

"Pretty sure." The two men rose to leave.

Jones looked over his glasses at Thompson. "My guess is…." he hesitated. "it came from the free clinic. That's where most of our written prescriptions come from now."

Thompson gave a slight nod as he followed Mac out the office door.

****

When they returned, a reporter from a regional television station was parked in Thompson's office. Elam was not surprised by the visit and waited while a cameraman took position before providing a brief rundown of the cases and answering generic questions from a young reporter who had little experience with law enforcement and even less knowledge of the case.

His wife would see him on the six o'clock news, the ten-minute interview cut to a thirty-second spot. She would invariably comment on how tired he looked.

When the office was clear of the reporter and the cameraman, Thompson joined Mac and Dolan in the conference room. They were now fully committed to the paperwork of the investigations. Printed phone records, files, and legal pads littered the table. Dolan was on the phone as he turned toward Thompson.

"I've got a few things to review as soon as he gets off the phone," Mac pointed at Dolan. The investigator finished his call as if on cue and sat across from Mac and Thompson.

"OK, what we got?" said Thompson.

Mac took the lead. "This is a list of hospital employees, reported overdoses in the last six months, and I have the owners of the two Ford trucks we saw in the hospital staff parking area."

"OK – let's start with the easy one first. Tell me about the trucks."

"Expensive vehicles, both top-of-the-line King Ranch models." Mac handed the one-page printout to Thompson. "Guess what—one belongs to our friendly hospital administrator, Ed Lang, and the other is registered to a nurse practitioner, Lloyd Rich. That's the darker one—kind of charcoal grey."

Thompson thought and said, "I think we can dismiss Lang for now. I don't like the guy, but he doesn't seem the type, plus he can't write prescriptions."

Dolan replied, "Yeah, but he could get access to a prescription pad."

Thompson pondered the idea for a moment. "That's true, but I just don't see it. Plus, all these drugs can't only be coming from prescriptions. Does anybody know this Rich fellow?"

No one responded.

Thompson continued. "I don't think he's local, or some of us would know him or his family. We'll have to find out a little bit more about Mr. Rich."

Mac offered, "I don't know anyone well enough who works at the hospital. I don't think anyone would be comfortable talking to me. We could have a go at Lang, but I don't think he would give us any more than he wanted us to know, and I believe the first thing he would do is tell Rich we're looking at him."

Yeah, let's keep Lang out of this for now. We may still have to look at him. I'll take care of it. I know just who to talk to."

"Now, the employee list. We don't really know what to look for – but how many pharmacists are there?"

Mac browsed the list. "It looks like there's only one on the payroll: Evan Winter. I'm not sure, but I think small hospitals use contract pharmacists for nights and weekends. They didn't give me a list of contract employees. I didn't think to ask. There are also two techs on the payroll."

"Wait a minute. I know Winter," Dolan added. "Lives a couple of blocks from me."

Thompson looked at Dolan, waiting for more.

"Probably mid-thirties, a little pudgy, kinda squirrelly, if you know what I mean."

"No, not exactly."

"Nervous fellow, friendly enough, but hard to carry on a conversation with. Now, his wife is a piece of work. She's a teacher over at the high school but dresses like she's high class…. She drives a top-of-the-line SUV… just kinda snooty. I think she rules the roost, if you know what I mean."

Mac wondered at Dolan's mild animosity toward a woman he hardly knew, but this was a small town. People needed something to talk about, and putting on airs above your station in life did little to endear one with those who placed little value on such things.

Dolan seemed to realize that maybe he had said too much. "Just an observation. I don't know her too well. Guess it ain't no crime to like to spend money."

Thompson quelled the awkward silence that followed. "I'll check him out too."

"Is there anything on the overdose list that might be useful?"

Mac took the pages from the table. "I haven't had a chance to look at it closely, but probably not. Jimmy recognized a few chronic users, but I can almost guarantee that most of these names are fake. Most of the bills were never paid. About half were treated with naloxone, some were just monitored or hydrated, and a few just walked out after stabilizing.

Thompson leaned forward. "Just so we're all on the same page, what is naloxone used for?"

Naloxone is the most common drug used for opioid overdose. I understand it's pretty effective. Most folks know it as Narcan or Kloxxado. Those are brand names. The problem for us is that it's used for street drugs like heroin and cocaine and for prescription overdoses of painkillers. We've got no way of knowing what drugs these folks were treated for and probably won't find them to ask."

Mac looked at Thompson before commenting further. "We'd probably waste a lot of time with little results if we try to chase these people down."

"OK, put it at the bottom of the pile, and we'll follow up if necessary. Dolan, get that warrant for me this afternoon and then drive over to Orangefield Road and talk to the Camfield boys. You probably won't get much out of them but find out if that was where Dean and Deeter hung out. You'll find out more from what they don't say than the pack of lies they're gonna tell ya."

Thompson stood and closed the file in front of him. "I got a man to see."

CHAPTER 23

Elam's thoughts jumped about. Like most people, personal issues always seemed to intrude into his workdays: from how to afford the new set of tires needed for Caroline's car to next week's doctor visit that would surely be unpleasant and back to the inventory of questions he was about to ask.

The drive was short, and he pulled into a long private road lined with large pines, smaller oaks, and hickory. A hundred yards in, the trees yielded to an expansive opening landscaped with azaleas, crepe myrtles, and other shrubs he couldn't name. The drive curved gracefully across the manicured landscape to the right of a large, modern brick home with two of the four garage doors open. He parked behind one of the closed doors and heard his name as he stepped out.

"Back here, Elam."

Behind the house, he saw a small red tractor with a front-end loader elevated waist high. Standing in front of the bucket was a man of sixty wearing a porkpie hat, a torn t-shirt, and cutoff jeans. A pair of white hairless legs smeared with dirt and sweat bottomed out in short rubber boots. As Elam approached, James Barton leaned against the loader bucket, his arms resting on the rim, his hands smoothing the mix of bark, sand, and topsoil inside.

"I thought a rich fella like you would hire this kind of work done, Doc." Thompson's eyes twinkled.

"Can't find anybody that'll satisfy my wife. She's already run off two landscapers this spring. Besides, I like to get my hands dirty now and again. I'm still a country boy at heart."

The yard had the feel and look of a much older southern estate—mature trees and shrubs, well-trimmed hedges aligning walkways leading to a pool area, and a small, aerated pond near the edge of the property.

"Appreciate you taking the time to talk to me, Doc. I need a little information about some folks at the hospital."

"Oh." Doc Barton took the hat from his head and slapped it against his thighs to remove any sand and dirt. "Well, come up to the porch here, and I'll have Rhonda fix us some lemonade."

They walked up a slight set of steps onto an arbored deck, where Elam took a seat in a cushioned wicker chair that probably cost more than all the furniture in his home.

Barton disappeared into the house but returned shortly with a tray containing two glasses full of ice and a large pitcher filled with lemonade. The pitcher was loaded with lemon slices and cherries.

As Barton poured, he asked, "Who do you wanna know about?"

"There's a lot of prescription drugs floating around out there, Doc. Too many for such a small town. We think they're connected to our murders."

"And you think it's connected to the hospital somehow?"

"We're just covering all our bases. I guess the drugs could be coming in from other places, but that's not likely – too small a market here, and there's a lot more demand and profit in the bigger cities, and probably easier to hide there."

"What about the pharmacies? You know there's..." He stopped for a moment and thought. "There's six of them in town."

"We'll be checking them out, too, but right now, I wanted to ask you about Evan Winter."

Barton reached into his glass, grabbed a cherry, popped it into his mouth, and pulled the stem. He shook his head. "I don't think so. Evan's too timid. He wouldn't have the nerve to do something like that... but then I guess he is one of those who could be talked into it. He would never do anything dangerous on his own, but he is pretty gullible."

"I hear he needs money to keep his wife in a "certain" lifestyle."

"I wouldn't know about that. I only know him professionally. We have a quarterly staff meeting to go over operating procedures and have our do better talks. I can't say we've had any major issues. The only thing I can think of is that the administrator had some questions about the volume of out-of-date drugs in the pharmacy last quarter, but it wasn't a big deal. Winters said he'd keep a closer eye on things, but I don't think anybody followed up on it. If you wanna know more about Winter, you probably should ask Lloyd Rich. They seem to be close."

Elam set his glass back down on the tray. "Rich, that's the other fellow I wanted to talk to you about. He's a nurse practitioner, ain't he? That means he can write prescriptions, right?"

"Yeah, some, anyway. Now, Rich is a piece of work. He's a good worker and always available for extra shifts if needed, but like I say, he's a piece of work."

"What do you mean?"

"Well, let me put it this way: He's been through most of the single women in town and a few of the married ones. He likes his ladies, his clothes, and likes to have a good time."

"Do you think he might write a few extra prescriptions now and then?"

"Hell, Elam, I don't know. I couldn't say something like that about a fella I don't know. He hasn't been here that long, maybe a year or eighteen months. Like I said, he does a good job. The rest isn't my concern unless you tell me it should be."

"Well, I ain't tellin' you that, at least not right now." Elam downed his glass and looked at it admiringly. "That's some fine lemonade, Doc."

"Ain't it, though."

"While I'm here, I might as well ask you: What do you think of Ed Lang, your administrator?"

Barton laughed. "He's an asshole, but he's our asshole. On the hospital board, we call him "Prune Juice" – just not to his face." He saw the perplexed smile on Elam's face.

"Prune juice – not too appealing, but if you don't take a dose of it now and then, you get backed up with crap. He's a damn good administrator. It's not a job that makes you popular, and Lang fits the bill."

Elam nodded. Considering his dislike for the man, he had hoped for a worse opinion. "One more thing. You said something about out-of-date drugs. I didn't know pills could go bad. What happens to those?"

"They don't necessarily go bad. Sometimes, they lose their effectiveness, but once they exceed the date set by the manufacturer, they have to be destroyed even if they're still good—incinerated. It's always a big loss for the hospital."

"Who is responsible for that?"

"It's Winter's job to identify and document them. The protocol requires a medical staff member to sign off on it and be present when they're destroyed."

"So, a doctor has to be present?"

"Or a registered nurse or nurse practitioner. It's not a normal job for anyone; nobody likes to do it." Barton smiled knowingly. "Come to think of it, Lloyd Rich has volunteered since he got here."

Elam absorbed the information and rose to leave. "I appreciate it, Doc. Sure is nice here – could sit here all afternoon."

"Well, why don't you? You're the boss, ain't you?"

"Yeah, but I want to stay the boss till I can get my pension. By the way, when are you going to retire? You're getting a little long in the tooth."

Barton poured another glass of lemonade and said, "When I get this place paid for and enough money in the bank to go to Europe twice a year."

***

Mac pulled into the gravel parking lot of the free clinic at 11:00 am and waited. The lot was nearly full when he arrived, but the cars had begun to thin out. He watched as people came and went, working-class men and women, older folks, and a few younger folks without the desire or the ability to pay for insurance or who were no longer carried on their parent's coverage. He recognized a few faces of those he had encountered through his work in law enforcement, those who sought out trouble or couldn't seem to avoid it.

He grabbed his cell and stepped out of the truck as Fugly Brown came out of a side door and headed toward an older silver compact. He jumped off the step and shook his hands over his head like a triumphant boxer before sliding into the passenger seat. Mac could not see the driver -only that it was a woman.

When he entered the clinic, he was greeted by a young volunteer who pointed out Lloyd Rich. Rich was walking the room looking over patients, searching for those in greatest need.

The building still looked much like a church sanctuary. Many of the pews had been removed, but others were positioned along the walls and in the center of the room. Each held one or two individuals. There was sufficient seating to allow them to sit apart, each hoping not to encounter something contagious or horrendous.

The volunteer waved Rich to the reception desk at the back of the structure. His demeanor was relaxed, and when he was introduced to Mac, a frozen and practiced smile never left his face. "It's a pleasure, Mr. McKenzie. What can I do for you?"

"I'm working on an investigation and would like a few words with you if possible."

"Sure. I've got time to handle two more patients before we close the doors – if you don't mind waiting a few minutes."

"Not a problem. Don't want to interfere with your work. I'll just take a seat."

Rich nodded and attended to an elderly lady with a walker, helping her rise and leading her through the door to the makeshift examining rooms. A few minutes later, he repeated the process with a pale young woman who couldn't be more than eighteen, two young children in tow.

One of the volunteers announced at noon that no more patients would be seen today. A written statement was then read aloud for insurance and liability purposes.

Volunteers man the free clinic, and its assets are provided by the nonprofit organization Buford Medical Trust. Neither the clinic nor its volunteers assume liability for your treatment. If you have serious medical needs, we highly recommend that you see a private physician or visit the emergency room at your local hospital. The clinic is open on Monday and Thursday from 8:00 am to noon. Services are free of charge, but donations are appreciated.

The waiting room was clear before the statement was completed. The doors were locked, and the administrative volunteers turned to their paperwork. It was ten more minutes before Lloyd Rich stuck his head through the doorway at the front of the room and waved at Mac.

He held the door for him and stated, "We have a small office three doors down on your left. We can talk in there."

The lighting was poor, and the hardwood floors rang under their feet. They were clean but lacking varnish. The walls were plastered with health posters about diabetes symptoms, high blood pressure, vaccination requirements, venereal diseases, and HIV.

The office was more modern, with better lighting, a polished wooden desk, and a pair of upholstered chairs. The artwork on the wall would have been better suited for a chain motel but did serve to brighten the room.

Mac took a seat in the nearest chair and said, "Thank you. I'll try not to take too much of your time."

"That's not a problem. I have about an hour of paperwork, but my shift at the hospital doesn't start until three. Now, what's this all about?" Rich eased into the chair behind the desk, leaned back, and placed his hands behind his head, a smile still on his lips.

Mac saw no value in being deceptive. "We're investigating the deaths of two young men, and there seems to be a prescription drug connection between them. We're checking with all the local physicians but wondered if they may have frequented the clinic here."

Rich frowned as if on cue. "Yeah, I heard about those boys – can't remember their names though, both kinda similar, weren't they?"

"Jason Deeter, 23, and Jason Dean, 26. Do you have any recollection of them?"

"I don't recognize the names, but maybe if I saw their faces. I have to be honest with you: I don't pay much attention to names. The folks up front check them in, and I just treat them. I've got no way of knowing for sure, but at a place like this, I suspect we get a lot of false names and false IDs. We get quite a few that claim they don't have any ID."

"You don't need an ID to write them a prescription?"

Rich paused for a moment and leaned into the desk. "Well, no, not really. If we're suspicious, maybe, but once they sign their paperwork, we generally assume they are who they say they are."

Mac reached into his shirt pocket and slid photos of the two men across the desk. "Both pictures are a couple of years old, but they haven't changed much."

Rich took a photo in each hand and looked at them intently. He held up the photo of Deeter and said, "This one looks familiar, but I can't say for sure. The other one, I don't recognize."

Mac hesitated with his next question, knowing what the answer would be. "Would it be possible to examine the records here? Maybe they were patients, and you don't remember, or they were treated by someone else."

Rich shook his head as if dealing with a kid full of childish desires. "I personally would have no objections, but that would have to be cleared by the medical trust's attorney. You know, we also fall under HIPPA, even if we are a free clinic. "

"I understand, we'll pursue that. Just for clarification, what is the Buford Medical Trust?"

"I wasn't here when it was formed, but it's a nonprofit set in place—it consists of the two largest churches in town and the hospital board. They saw a need; the hospital emergency room was always overflowing and losing money. I'll have to say it works pretty well, but we still can't treat everybody who needs it."

"So, you're a volunteer?"

"Yes, sir, just like everybody else here. I'm a fortunate man, and I feel like I should give something back. I'm paid well at the hospital, so I don't feel like a few hours a week is too much to ask of me."

Mac now asked a typical southern small-town question. "You're not from around here, are you?"

"No, sir, I'm from the outskirts of Memphis. Moved here about a year and a half ago. I've got no family. My mom died while I was in school. I thought I'd go somewhere where I was needed. I first thought about the Delta, but it was just too damned depressing over there, but I like it here."

Mac turned the conversation. "What do you typically treat here?"

Rich leaned back again, a smile returning to his face. "Nothing major, I promise you that. Mostly, we treat people who won't go to a doctor because of the cost. We have regulars that we treat for diabetes and high blood pressure. We do a few stitches, pain relief for arthritis, colds, and flu, light injuries—that kind of stuff. Anything major, we send right off to the hospital. We're kind of like the old military triage."

He paused and looked directly at Mac. "But I don't suppose that's what you're interested in?"

"No, not really."

"Pain killers, Oxycontin, Vicodin, stuff like that, I suppose. Well, we do prescribe these, but only in cases of extreme and obvious pain and rarely more than once. If we genuinely believe they need a regimen of painkillers, we encourage them to see a private physician and send them on their way.

"Do you keep these drugs here?"

Rich became more cautious, and his ever-present smile cracked slightly." Not in any quantity. We've had two break-ins just since I've been here. That has to be what they're looking for. There's obviously little cash here. No, most of the drugs here are samples provided by the pharmaceutical companies."

"These break-ins….," Mac said. "Did they get away with any drugs?"

"One did—about three months ago. A police report was filed with Seymore PD. They should have a full inventory."

"Is it possible that they might have also stolen some prescription pads? We're getting reports of fake prescriptions at local pharmacies, and there is some indication that they come from here."

Rich's demeanor shifted abruptly. "My God, I never thought of that." His voice lowered, and he looked toward the door to the office. "Mr. McKenzie, I have to tell you, some of our folks get pretty lax, and the last thing you want to report is a lost pad."

He leaned in closer and placed his hands on the desk. "We're an all-volunteer staff, but some are more volunteer than others if you know what I mean. I work just about every shift here, but most of the others rotate in and out. Some of them don't want to be here but get a lot of pressure from the hospital. They resent it, and sometimes they're not as careful as they should be."

Mac nodded. "Anybody particular?"

Rich did not hesitate. "No, sir. And if there were, I wouldn't say. I've got no evidence or even a suspicion of anyone. I'm just saying it's possible."

Mac did not respond but reached into his pocket for his keys. "Just a couple more questions. Do you get a lot of... I don't know what you call it... pill shopping? Folks looking to score some medication."

Rich nodded. "Oh, yeah. It happens almost every day. It's mostly young people, but not all. They're usually easy to spot. They almost always have some problem without obvious symptoms—back pain, usually. We're trained to weed them out."

"I see." Mac looked at Rich intently to gauge his reaction. "I saw Fugly Brown coming out as I was going in. He wouldn't be one of those "shoppers," would he?"

Mac saw an almost imperceptible change in the man at the mention of Fugly.

"Fugly? That's a new one."

"You probably know him as Alan Brown, skinny redheaded kid."

"OK – sure. He was here. Mr. Brown has been here in the past. I don't think I should say more except he was here this time about his kid."

Rich broadened that smile and stood. "I hope I've been of some help to you, but I need to get to that paperwork."

"Of course." Mac rose, headed toward the door, opened it halfway, and said, "One more thing. Do you know Evan Winter?"

***

It was one of those rare low-humidity days. The air was clear and light, and the sounds of the town sang with a clarity not usually heard in the throes of summer. By July, the chance of such a day was all but nil. The lightness of the atmosphere and the slight cooling brought a spring to the step of old men like him—including those who gathered at the breakfast bars drinking lousy coffee, debating politics and telling lies, or those who sat with indifference in front of the courthouse.

Such days should be embraced and remembered, but rarely were. Mac regretted that he had spent the better part of the morning in the free clinic and would spend the rest of the day trading notes with the Sheriff and pouring over phone records.

Before returning to the courthouse, he headed home for a late lunch with Mary. As he walked into the kitchen, he found a plate covered with a dish towel and a note on the counter.

"Going to pick up some meds for Miss Sweet. See you this evening."

He uncovered the plate of home-grown tomato slices, sliced onion, butter beans, and cornbread. Pouring a glass of iced tea, he sat at the kitchen table.

The case was becoming more complicated each day. He knew that a proper investigation would require warrants; plenty of warrants, for the pharmacies, the free clinic, and probably the hospital as well, not to mention any additional phone records if more information should develop.

The whole thing puzzled him. Yeah, there were drugs involved and a considerable amount, but not the amount and not the type to be expected of any local large-scale drug operation. It just didn't seem like the type of situation that would result in the deaths of two men. Murder would lead to too much attention. The amount of money involved didn't justify such drastic action.

Maybe this was more personal. Maybe Dean and Deeter were skimming off the top or holding back on some of the drugs and selling them themselves. If they worked directly for some big players, they would likely be too afraid to do that. These kids were small-scale. One had served some time, and one was known as a troublemaker, but neither could be classified as a hardened criminal. Neither had shown a tendency toward violence. Whoever they were dealing with didn't instill a great deal of fear in them. Maybe they even felt their supplier had too much to lose to take any action against them. They may have even resorted to blackmail to up their supply. So, who would be subject to blackmail? Someone with a position or status in the community.

A big player might have sent someone to teach these guys a lesson. The twenty-two and the bullets to the head did look like a well-planned hit, but those guys were more careful. They would not have wanted the publicity or the scrutiny of a murder investigation. They might have roughed them up a bit, broken a bone, or threatened their family members, but the killings seemed excessive.

By the time he sopped the last bite of cornbread in the combined juices on his plate, he had convinced himself that there was a personal aspect to this case. He rinsed off his plate in the sink, poured out his ice, and scribbled a message to Mary on the bottom of her note before heading out the door.

CHAPTER 24

Small Southern towns are hotbeds for characters. Such places encourage them, celebrate them, and hold them up for the world to see, often placing them in all their glory on the front porch, the steps of the courthouse, or the public benches of the town square. Most are treated with a level of sympathetic respect and seen as adding color to an often drab and mundane existence.

There was usually a back story, known to only a few, that gave some insight into these personalities, but most folks just took them as they were and used their occasional encounters as fodder for conversation over the evening dinner table.

On a regular basis, the Buford Sheriff's office or the Seymore police had to deal with at least one of these oddballs. It was usually a simple matter; a misunderstanding, an agitation, or an indiscretion easily resolved when a uniform became involved.

Old Joe was Elam Thompson's burden to bear; even within the city limits of Seymore, Thompson was called whenever Joe caused a ruckus. Today was no exception. "Elam, you need to come get old Joe!"

Old Joe bragged that he was a descendant of Confederate General Stephen D. Lee on his mother's side. To hear him tell it, he was quite a man. He was in possession of the smartest dog across four states. Each year, he grew the biggest watermelons and the finest tomatoes of anyone in the county. He made the best barbecue with dubious meats, and he always shot the largest buck and caught the biggest fish every season.

Joe was also a health expert. He had remedies for everything from shingles to toe fungus and backaches. He firmly believed that excessive bathing was the number one cause of cancer, heart disease, and most other ills; something about leeching the essential oils from the skin needed to fight off infection. He, therefore, boasted that he chose to only bathe at the changing of the seasons. Most folks were dubious of his claims except for the latter.

Old Joe rambled about the town and countryside in a Chevy pickup, the bed full of beer cans, plastic trash bags full of indeterminate debris, old batteries, busted concrete blocks, pieces of two-by-fours, and bald tires. The truck's age and model were anyone's estimate due to missing bumpers, mirrors, and a tailgate - its body, a landscape of dents, holes, rust, and Bondo.

Joe lived in an old house about five miles from town, left to him by his mother. There were reports that at least one of the back rooms had collapsed, and there was no functioning plumbing. He never seemed to have a job as he could be found at any time of day arguing over prices or attempting to barter junk at the feed store, grocery store, or a local hardware store.

Thompson pulled into the parking lot of Delmer's E-Z Go convenience store on the edge of town to find Joe standing behind his truck near the entrance, engaged in a shouting match with a young girl with blue hair standing in the half-open door. The girl paused when she saw Thompson and said slightly under her breath, "Finally!"

Thompson motioned to the girl. "Go back inside. I'll be right there." He turned to Joe and raised both his hands, palms out. "I don't want to hear it. Go sit in your truck till I get out of the store."

Joe wanted to protest, but Thompson shook his hands at him again, and he reluctantly opened the driver's door and sat down.

When Thompson entered the store, he found the woman behind the counter pulling her multicolored hair into a ponytail, the anger still visible on her face.

"What did he do this time?"

"I've just about had it with him, Sheriff. He drives up here in that old piece of crap and pumps gas and then comes in here and tries to pay for it with some junk out of the back of his truck. When I wouldn't let him, he goes outside and starts pissing all over the ice cooler and the walls of the building. That's when I had enough and called the cops."

Thompson couldn't help but smile, which the woman obviously did not appreciate. "He didn't threaten you or get violent in any way, did he?"

"No, sir, but he did cuss at me, and I ain't going to take that from nobody."

"OK, I'm going to get the money for the gas and send him out of here. Will that be ok with you?"

"Yes, sir, but tell him not to come back - at least not when I'm working."

Joe was leaning against the edge of his truck seat, his feet on the ground, sockless feet in a pair of old leather shoes without laces. The body odor and the stench from the truck made Thompson stand back a few feet.

With a hangdog expression, Joe said, "Elam, I didn't do nothin'. That girl's half-crazy; you see that hair she's got?"

"She says you wouldn't pay for your gas, and then you came out here and pissed all over the place. You know you can't do that."

"I tried to pay for the gas, but she wouldn't let me. And when a man's gotta go, he's gotta go. It ain't healthy to hold your water. Causes all them toxicities to build up in your body."

Thompson shook his head. " How much was the gas?"

"$15, but I ain't got it. I'll have it next week, but I ain't got it right now."

Thompson didn't step any closer but waved his finger at him. "Get on out of here, and don't come back anytime soon. And if you see that girl behind the counter, don't come back at all. You bring that $15 by my office sometime next week, or I'll come looking for it."

Joe cackled as he crawled in and cranked his truck. "I knew you was a good ol' fella. I'll be by next week, I promise. Yes sir, a good ol' fella."

Thompson watched the old rattletrap head down the street toward the town square. He had some feelings of guilt that he had not issued any number of citations for that truck, but the fact that Joe never drove it more than 30 miles an hour and the possible loss of any goodwill that helped him deal with the man on a regular basis had prevented him from doing so. He walked back inside, pulled $15 from his wallet, and handed it to the girl.

Fugly Brown had been watching the whole episode from one of the booths near the front window of the store. He had been trying to make himself inconspicuous and hoped the Sheriff would not see him.

Thompson had spotted him before he even got out of the truck. He turned to him before he walked out and said, "You got anything new for me, Fugly?"

Fugly stubbed out a cigarette and said, "No, sir. Ain't hardly been out of the apartment- babysitting, you know. But as soon as I can, I'll do some checking for you."

Thompson stared at him for a moment and said, "You ain't supposed to be smoking in here," before walking out the door and heading back to the office.

CHAPTER 25

The back door to the Sheriff's office had been propped open with a concrete block to allow in the fresh air and sunlight. No one seemed to mind the slight odor of tobacco smoke that wafted in from the benches just outside the door. Mac found Thompson seated in his chosen spot, a cell phone plastered to his ear and a half-smoked cigarette between the fingers of his other hand.

"Well, look... I've got to go. I know you're worried about it, and I'll send John Luke out to talk to you this afternoon. I'll come out myself and talk to him as soon as I can, but it may be a day or so." He paused, pulled the phone back from his ear, and shook his head at Mac as he listened to the response. "I understand. We'll take care of it."

He set the phone on the bench beside him and looked at Mac. "The biggest mistake I ever made was to give my personal phone number to some of our more prominent citizens in this county. Did you find anything interesting at the clinic?"

"Just a lot more questions. Did you know they've had a couple of burglaries there in the last few months?"

"No, I didn't. I assume some drugs were involved."

"In least one of them. I'll go to the Police Department this afternoon and get the reports. By the way, I thought you might find this interesting. I saw Fugly Brown coming out as I was going in, and he was a happy man."

"Uh-huh."

"Yep, looked like he just won the lottery. As happy as a puppy with two peckers."

"Now, that doesn't sound like a normal reaction when you're coming out of the free clinic. Must have got a clean bill of health."

"Maybe, but I wouldn't bet on it. I think we had better be looking hard at this Rich fellow."

"Yeah, his name does keep popping up. Did you find out anything from him?"

"He's slick—too slick. He had all the right answers and all the right excuses. He said a prescription pad could have been stolen in the robberies but not reported. He made a point of the idea that some of his fellow volunteers were not too careful."

"Well, that could be."

"True. When I mentioned Fugly Brown, I could see there was a little reaction from him. When I asked him how well he knew Evan Winter at the hospital, he gave me the standard song and dance. He said he knew him and liked him well enough, but they weren't close personal friends."

Thompson lit another cigarette. "Well, that kind of conflicts with what my sources tell me. I understand they're pretty close."

"It may be just because I don't like the guy, but I would lay odds that he's involved somehow."

"Rubbed you the wrong way, did he?"

"My daddy told me never to trust a man that smiles all the time. His looked like it was painted on."

Thompson nodded and inhaled deeply before throwing his cigarette butt into the drywall bucket. "I'll have Jimmy run a background check on him. Let's go inside and see where we are on those warrants."

Dolan was sucking down coffee and searching through the empty donut boxes on the conference table when they entered. He straightened and threw the Styrofoam cup into the trash. "Just coming out to get you, Boss. I talked to the judge, and he gave us a limited warrant just for the prescription made out to the girl. I could tell he was a little worried about issuing a warrant related to medical records. He said once we find her prescription and it leads to something else, then come back and talk to him. He also suggested that it might be in our best interest to talk to the District Attorney and run any warrants through him."

Thompson knew the judge was right concerning the DA but didn't relish the idea. He had briefed him on Monday but had no further communication since then. He didn't have much more to tell him, and he dreaded the extra layer of bureaucracy it would entail. He nodded at Dolan to acknowledge the point and turned to Mac. "Let's get everything lined up and follow up all the leads we've got right now before I give him a call. What about that police report on the free clinic burglaries?"

"I'll run over there right now and get copies. Shouldn't take long."

Thompson turned back to Dolan. "Take that warrant over to Jergens Pharmacy and get that prescription for me. He's cooperative, so it shouldn't take too long. Have him make a copy but bring the original prescription to me. I'll meet both of you back here about 4:30, and we'll see what we got."

When the investigators left, Thompson entered his office, pulled off his boots, and leaned back in his chair. Soon, he was sound asleep.

Both men returned by 4:00. Seeing that Thompson was asleep, Dolan and Mac looked at each other before settling into the conference room to trade notes.

Mack noticed that Dolan seemed antsy and distracted and discovered that his boy had a ball game that afternoon.

"There's no reason for you to miss that game. I'll give Elam the prescription and brief him on everything, and we'll catch up tomorrow."

Dolan beamed and immediately headed for the door. "I appreciate that. My boy's gonna pitch today. I'd hate to miss that."

At 4:30, Mack knocked on the office door and roused a groggy Thompson. "You look tired. These cases keeping you up at night?"

"That's part of it, I guess." Elam had grown to like Mac. He liked his calm manner and the logic he applied to everything he did. He put him at ease. He stood up and looked out the window behind his desk.

"I've got a doctor's appointment next week, and I already know what he's gonna tell me. I bought a diabetes test kit last week. My blood sugar's been hovering around 300."

Mac whistled. "That's pretty high. Stress makes it worse."

183

Thompson continued looking out the window, his back to Mac. "I've got twenty-two years in. I started working in the police force when I was just a kid. I need to finish this term and one more before I can get a decent pension. Days like these make me wonder if it's worth it or not. I don't know if I can continue to do a good job."

Max settled into a chair, placed the paperwork on the desk, and crossed his legs. "You're at a tough age. I see it in a lot of men. Been there myself. The responsibilities start to pile up, and you haven't quite reached the point in your career where you have real security, but you have reached the point where you got to start taking care of yourself: eating better and finding ways to deal with the stress - I'll give a little fatherly advice if you don't mind."

Thompson turned around with a curious expression and nodded his head.

"You're going to have to find little pockets of peace to dive into from time to time. This life demands too much of some folks and too little of others. When I was a younger man like you, I only had one hope for old age – that things would be settled, that I could face infirmity with a peaceful mind. We're naïve even as the grown men we are, doing the kind of work we do.

I'm not at peace, but I sometimes feel it in my bones. Not that I believe any man can achieve peace on this earth. It's too far ahead of us in our youth, and there's too much debris behind and around us when we're older; that stuff of life that we keep picking up and examining, thinking we'll find some answer there and all the while it's always just beyond us over that next hill."

He stopped for a moment to see if he should continue - if Thompson might think he was just a rambling old fool.

"I'm basically an old man now. I would have been considered ancient in this profession a few generations back. It's a blessing and a curse. I'm not talking so much about the physical aspects of it. That's what we all seem to be consumed by. Always looking for that magic pill needed to keep our youth just a little bit longer. I can't do what I used to, but I'm generally ok with that. I don't dwell on it even if I do have a few bouts of depression and regret that I can't climb up on my roof anymore or sleep through the night."

"But as I get older, I am consumed by a need to understand people. If you're a thinking man, age brings the ability to understand folks more - to see their strengths but mostly their weaknesses. As a result, you have to face your own. I look at all these weaknesses I've carried inside me all my life—judgments and actions based on the wrong things, accepting the wrong influences. There's always something gnawing at you, back behind you, waiting to pounce in the dark, and it scares the hell out of you. Like a dream that you can't quite remember - the why of it all that leaves you uneasy."

Thompson nodded and seemed to be listening, so he continued.

"We spend most of our lives trying to place blame for our shortcomings, where and when we were born, the qualities missing in our parents, the opportunities missed when we were in the wrong place at the wrong time, society's prejudices and social structure. But in reality, our shortcomings are our own. Age brings the knowing - knowing that you were just too lazy, too desirous, too scared and confused by the world around you, too unwilling to examine and pursue the right thing or lacking the ability to know what the right thing is."

"I see a young man, someone like Fugly Brown, and I'm torn between envy and pity. He has an ability that men like you and me can never possess. He can take his conscience and shove it deep down into his bowels, where it does little more than yield a belly ache when he hits a woman or sticks a needle in his arm. He ain't tormented by it or directed by it. But then I pity him because he'll never know or see any true level of peace. He can't recognize it. He'll shorten his life, harden his soul, and yield any joy of living to his weaknesses. That's just the way it is for men like him. His lifestyle will eventually kill him, but it's the stress of trying to be a better man that will kill you if you don't learn to deal with it."

Mac slumped slightly when he finished, embarrassed at his presumption that Thompson needed advice and his own need to give it.

Thompson smiled and sat back down in his chair. "Wow, that was a speech. It was pretty good, too."

Mac nodded and looked out the window. "Been practicing it for years. I never got to give it to my own boy. I probably should have just told you to buy yourself a good pair of walking shoes and take up fishing."

Thompson reached across the desk without comment and picked up the papers, an indication that he didn't want to discuss his personal issues further.

He looked closely at the prescription, clearly marked with a watermark and the name Buford Medical Trust – Free Clinic. The handwriting was consistent; the patient's name, the drug and dosage prescribed, and the signature were all made with the same hand. He handed it to Mac. "Everything's legible except the signature. What does that look like to you?"

Mac held it and examined it just like he had previously. "It could be Louis Rich, but then again, it could be something else. We'll have to get the names of all the doctors and practitioners who have worked in the clinic lately just to be sure… not that I think it's going to matter. There is no doubt in my mind that someone will discover that a prescription pad is missing, and the signature won't match anyone at the clinic."

Thompson sighed dejectedly. "It looks like we're going to need a sack full of warrants for this one, which means it's going to take time. I think we've got enough to get paper for the clinic's records and warrants for the local pharmacies, at least related to any prescriptions coming from the clinic."

"What about the hospital and maybe Rich's financials?"

"I don't think we have enough to convince a judge on those. We don't have anything on Rich, and nothing indicates that someone at the hospital is involved. Maybe what we find at the clinic will break that loose."

Mac grunted. "And all that's going to do is confirm what we already know – that at least some of these drugs are coming from the clinic. We need to talk to the pharmacist at the hospital, Winter. I have a hard time believing that all these drugs are coming just from fraudulent prescriptions."

Thompson considered this for a moment. "Yeah. Can you do that tomorrow?"

Mac nodded and said, "I can, but it'll be after lunch. I have a church board meeting in the morning."

"What about the police reports on the clinic break-ins? Have you got anything there"?

Mac handed a manila folder across the desk. "Just what you'd expect. The first one was just an attempted break-in. Broke a window and tried to pop the lock on the side door. The second one was more successful. They got a few dollars out of a cash box, a laptop, and a small amount of drugs. They did know what they were doing – all the drugs were schedule two- about $2000 worth as inventory, probably ten to fifteen thousand on the street."

"No missing prescription pads?"

"Not on the list."

Thompson rose and dropped the reports on his desk. "I suppose you'll also need to talk to the administrator tomorrow. That's going to stir the pot. Small-town politics; nobody wants any bad press or anything negative to surface about one of our biggest employers. There'll be some political pressure coming down on us once he gets his tights in a bunch." He looked down at the reports, a sour expression on his face. "Ask him about any audits on the pharmacy, and let's see how he responds."

CHAPTER 26

She'd been on him all day since she had arrived home from work and found the empty pizza box, the beer in the fridge, and the new Xbox console that he had barely gotten out of the packaging. It went downhill from there. At first, he had all but ignored her; the excitement of his new toy and the mellow mood produced by the first couple of beers had softened his responses, but as the barrage continued and the beers disappeared, his rage tightened his throat and buzzed in his head.

"Ain't no woman gonna tell me what to do. So, what if I spent a little money? I was the one that got it. I just wanna relax a little bit. I got some hard days coming."

"That ain't what you said. You said that money was for the baby and now look at you. What've you already spent? A thousand dollars, I bet. You know how much formula we could buy with a thousand dollars… and the diapers. Your boy goes through diapers like you go through beer. Give me the money and quit acting like a child. If you were half a man, you'd take that kid's toy back to the store and get the money back!"

Fugly snapped, his anger overwhelmed him, and he jumped up, strode around the couch to face her, his hand raised to strike. She never reacted but just coolly looked at him, a slight smile on her face. He lowered his hand and glowered at her.

With a hard calm in her voice, she said, "If you hit me, you'd better kill me or knock me out because I'll be calling that sheriff. The two years you got coming will turn into five."

Fugly dropped his shoulders, and his whole body slumped, his rage and pride in submission. He turned and sat on the ragged couch next to the game console and grabbed one of the controllers, fondling it before lighting a cigarette.

She looked at him without moving, an odd mix of disgust and pity on her face.

He spoke softly. "I weren't gonna hit you. I ain't never hit a woman."

"That's probably only cause you ain't ever had a woman but me, and now you know what'd happen if you did hit me."

She sighed, her anger easing. She couldn't understand the emotions that this man-boy stirred in her. On the surface and in her head, she had little hope for him or a relationship. She had expected him to blow the money, and she had little expectation that he would ever take any real responsibility for the boy. Yet maybe there was something, some tiny seed of decency, some backbone that she could find. She moved forward to touch his shoulders from behind the couch, removed his ever-present cap, and tousled his hair.

"You ain't a good man, Fugly. You ain't no bad man, but you ain't no good one either. I won't keep living like this, hoping for you to somehow be a good man. I don't know if you got it in you. I don't know exactly what's going on with you and that fellow from the clinic, but I know it's gonna cause trouble for you and maybe me too."

He reached up behind, took her hand, and placed it on his shoulder without looking at her. "I'll get you some more money."

She tousled his hair again. She looked about the shabbily furnished apartment and thought of all the bills she had to pay on a fast-food worker's salary.

"So, what is this "Call of Duty" thing you been talking so much about?"

CHAPTER 27

Darkness comes late in the summer in Mississippi. City kids play ball or walk the streets until after the streetlights hum to life. Farm kids venture along creek banks and the wood lanes until darkness forces them home to wash off the dust or the mud before reluctantly ending the day.

Buford County was very much a rural place. It didn't suffer from proximity to a larger town or a center of commerce. It was not infected with urban sprawl and the traffic of four-lane highways. Even though daylight lingers, city streets and country roads are rarely traveled after 8:00 p.m.

Louis Rich hated the slow pace and the lack of nightlife, but it served his purpose now. He had not encountered a single vehicle once he turned off the main highway.

When he first arrived in the area many months ago, he spent long afternoons riding the back roads of the county, finding hidden places of interest: empty decaying homes with yards overgrown with weeds, vacant since the sixties or before, old, abandoned barns, pullouts to creek banks used by the occasional fisherman and a jumbled network of unpaved trails.

As he drove, the woods seemed to close tighter and tighter, allowing only spangles of light through their canopy. Fifteen miles in and three increasingly narrow roads later, he turned onto a hidden lane, barely broad enough for a single vehicle. Low-hanging branches scraped the truck as he wound between the trees and made his way toward an opening two hundred yards in.

Evan Winter's dark sedan was parked next to a cabin of chaotic construction: a roof of rusty tin and walls made of a mix of board and batten, tin, and cheap siding cast off from construction sites. The clearing was scattered with an assortment of lean-tos, ancient campers, open barrels, and small sheds.

Rich pulled next to the sedan and rolled down his window. He noticed that Winter's car was still running, his radio at low volume.

"Turn that off so we can hear each other. I don't want to have to get out."

Winters turned off the radio and the car engine. He sat low in his seat, carrying the look of a frightened and defeated man.

"Why'd we have to meet out here? It's damned spooky in these woods."

Rich ignored the question. "Nobody knows you're here, right? What about your wife?"

"Hell, no. I told her I had to work late." Winter swallowed hard and turned toward Rich, peering over the door panel and trying to make out his features in the near darkness.

Rich hung his arm out the side window. "Like I said before, it's better that we are not seen together, especially now."

"What do you mean... especially now?"

Rich stared straight ahead through the windshield. "I had a visit from a cop today."

Winter's reaction was sheer panic. "God, I knew it." He pounded the steering wheel with the palm of his hands. "I can't go to jail, man. I'll never make it in there."

Rich was pleased at how well he had gauged the situation. Winter's hysteria was precisely what he wanted.

"Relax, you just need to keep your head about you. They don't know anything. It was an old dude from the Sheriff's Department, and he was just looking for information. I think they believe the drugs are coming from the clinic, and I might have even convinced them they're coming from a robbery. I don't think they suspect you or me, but I'm sure they will talk to you. Probably tomorrow."

Rich turned and looked directly at Winters. "I told you to take that fishing trip."

Winter was shaken, his eyes wide with fear. He stammered, "I don't have but a couple of vacation days left. We were leaving tomorrow after work. I was going to take Monday off. Maybe I can call in sick tomorrow."

Rich shook his head. "That will only look suspicious, and they'll probably just come to your house. You don't want Lucy to know about this. You just need to calm down. We discussed what to do if this happened; you just need to follow the plan."

Rich's first words were chosen to create trust. Now, it was time to create fear.

"You're not the only one in that pharmacy. They'll be looking at everyone, but you're in charge. It'll probably take a few days, but they'll get a warrant to look at your records and inventory. We've got to stick together on this, or we're both looking at some hard time."

A balloon of panic expanded in Winter's chest. Images of orange jumpsuits, gang rape, and public humiliation raced across his brain.

"Jesus. I grew up here, man. This will kill my folks and Lucy… Lucy will divorce me on the spot."

Rich feigned compassion. "You're a wreck, man. You got to calm down. You can handle this." On cue, he reached into the truck's console and appeared to root about for something of importance.

"Here." Across the space between the car and truck, he handed him a butterscotch pill bottle and then reached into the passenger seat for a bottle of water. 'Take two of those now and use the rest tomorrow to calm your nerves if you need them. We've got to talk and plan right now, but you're too upset."

Winter looked at the bottle, opened the top, and recognized the pills inside for what they were. Without hesitation, he turned the bottle up to his mouth and dropped two on his tongue before reaching for the water extended to him.

Rich said, "Now let's just talk for a few minutes till you -calm down, and we can work out a plan and what you need to say tomorrow."

Winters shook his head and stared out the windshield of the sedan. For the first time, but only for a moment, he became aware of the hum of night insects and the close call of a whippoorwill, pleasant sounds of his childhood while visiting his grandparents' farm on the other side of the county.

Rich began speaking in a low tone without inflection or change of pitch. He droned on about remaining calm and how there was little to worry about if the records were kept as he had been told.

It was now dark, and he could no longer see Winter's face, but he watched for movement. There was none. He waited five more minutes in silence to see if there was any response before exiting the car.

He used the flashlight app on his iPhone to illuminate Winter's face. The man's lips were blue, a small amount of foam in the corner of his mouth. His eyes rolled back in his head. Reaching back into his truck, he extracted a pair of medical gloves, a microfiber cloth, and a stethoscope. He checked the man's heart and respiration. Satisfied, he pulled the pill bottle and cap from between Winter's legs and wiped it down before pressing the man's right hand and fingers across it. He then repeated the process with the water bottle and placed it in a cupholder in the console. He took an envelope from his shirt pocket and tossed it into the passenger seat before examining the interior of the car. He popped the latch on the trunk and rooted about for anything that might connect him to Winters before returning to the driver's window.

Just to be sure, he placed the stethoscope against the man's chest and carotid artery before tossing the instrument into his truck. He took a moment and looked at the dead face before patting him on the arm through the car window. "Lucy was going to divorce you anyway."

He started his truck, turned around in the narrow space between the trees and the cabin, and drove back out the narrow lane before turning on his headlights.

CHAPTER 28

On Friday morning, the humidity and the heat returned to a torrid level. A front had moved through; rain was expected by late afternoon and predicted to continue throughout the weekend.

Thompson's arrival at the office was delayed when he stopped at a small country store for a breakfast biscuit. A couple of morning regulars bent his ear about a pack of dogs roaming the area, chasing cattle and killing an old lady's wiener dog in her front yard. The county lacked an animal control officer, and it was his department's responsibility to remedy the situation.

He pondered who he could spare on his staff to chase down a bunch of feral mutts as he drove into town, his air conditioning at full blast.

When he arrived, Dolan was sitting in his office. Before he could remove his gun and holster, Dolan waved a paper at him. "I got the info on that cell phone—where it was sold, I mean."

"Yeah, you gonna tell me or what?" His mood was soured by his morning encounter.

Dolan stared at him before saying, 'Truck stop on I-55 just south of Memphis, near Hernando."

Thompson stared at Dolan and waited for more.

"It's all there on the paper." He held it toward Thompson.

"Well, why don't you just tell me?" Thompson's patience was thinned by fatigue and stress. He tapped his computer keyboard to bring his screen to life and began searching for the reports he would need in the court session that would start within the hour.

Dolan withdrew the paper and examined it as he spoke. "Sold May 12th at 8:38 p.m. The cell phone company says it wasn't activated until the following day. And here's the best part. The truck stop does have video footage back until May 1st, and they'll let us look at it, but somebody's gotta go up there."

Thompson looked up from the screen. It was a four-hour drive to the Tennessee line, meaning he would lose an officer for the day. He couldn't send just an errand boy. He needed a deputy with some knowledge of security systems and computer files.

"Where's Jimmy?"

"Right here." Jimmy Smith stood in the doorway, his legs crossed and his hands in his pocket.

Thompson looked at him and smiled for the first time that morning. "You heard?"

Jimmy nodded. "I suppose you want me to go?"

"Yep. Take your laptop and a thumb drive. I want a copy of anything important. You know the questions to ask. If you leave now, you'll get back in time for a late supper."

Jimmy said, "Is there any other kind?"

Thompson didn't respond to the remark but said, "Take the SUV."

The county's newest vehicle, equipped with all the bells and whistles, the SUV was a source of contention within the department and was usually assigned to Dolan as the chief investigator.

Jimmy's excitement mushroomed across his face as he said, "Yes, sir." He tossed his patrol car keys to Dolan and held out his hand for the SUV keys.

As he turned to walk out the door, Thompson shouted after him. "Oh, and I don't expect any calls from the highway patrol about one of my vehicles doing a hundred miles per hour up the interstate."

The young officer just grinned as he headed to his office.

Thompson turned back to Dolan, who had an expression of concern on his face.

"I do something to piss you off, Boss?

Elam immediately regretted his gruffness with the man and shook his head. "No. Just had a bad start to the day, and as far as the vehicle is concerned, you're probably not going to need it today anyway."

He motioned for him to sit down. "I'm tied up in youth court all day. I need you to get with Judge Rickers and work on some warrants for the records at the free clinic and all the local pharmacies. It won't be easy. They'll probably have to be pretty specific, or he won't grant them. We need to know the names of anyone who can write prescriptions that worked at the clinic in the last six months, and we'll need to see the prescriptions or the logs for all schedule 2 drugs written from the clinic."

Dolan was taking quick notes but looked up questionably.

"I know, I know. We're pushing it, but work on him. Take the report on that girl- what's her name- Triste, and the prescription and the police report on the clinic break-in and see what you can do. We'll call the DA in if we have to, but it's just gonna delay things. Remind Judge Rickers that we've got two dead men, and the prescription drugs seem to be what ties them together."

Dolan grunted as he rose from the chair and said, "I'll see what I can do."

He paused further and stuck a pen behind his ear. "I'm getting backlogged on some of my other cases."

"I know. Can't be helped. When Jimmy gets back, pawn some of them off on him. And send John Luke in here before I go upstairs. He needs to talk to a man about some dogs.... and one more thing, tell Lindon to clean that damn coffee pot."

***

The young male receptionist at the hospital administrator's office looked confused when Mac asked for Evan Winter.

"Why would you look for him here?"

"Well, he works here, doesn't he?"

The man was prematurely balding. He ran his hand across the top of his head and held it before his eyes, looking for loose hairs. "Yes, sir, but he's not here. He didn't show up for work this morning. Wait – his wife didn't send you?"

"No."

"Well, I'm confused. His wife called this morning and said he didn't come home last night. I just assumed she filed a report with you."

"No. I don't know anything about that. I just wanted to talk with him about an investigation I'm working on."

The man shook his head and said, "I don't know what to tell you. You should probably talk to his wife."

Mac stared at him, trying to determine just how much information he could get from him. "Does he miss work often?"

"No, sir. I don't think so, but I wouldn't know for sure."

"How about his home address and a telephone number?"

"I suppose that would be ok." He turned to his computer and typed a few moments before writing down an address and two phone numbers on a scratch pad.

Mac took it and then asked, "Is Mr. Lang in today?"

"No, sir. He's at a convention in Biloxi and won't be back until Tuesday."

Mac nodded and tucked the slip of paper in his shirt pocket. "Thanks for the information."

"I hope everything's ok."

"I'm sure it is."

As Mac left the office, the young man watched him as he exited the building and walked across the parking lot before picking up the phone and dialing.

The address was for a newer subdivision in north Seymore, full of cookie-cutter houses with two-car garages and brick veneer across the front. The lawns were manicured, and the trees were limited and too immature to provide shade.

On the ride from the hospital, Mac dialed the first number on the scratch pad, only to find that it went to voice mail after four rings; actually, the recorded message indicated. *"We're sorry, this number has a voice mail box that is full. Please try again later."*

Evan Winter's house was on the front edge of a cul-de-sac and looked like every other home on the street. Builders tended to simply reverse the garages and change the number and location of false dormers to break the roofline.

He pulled into the drive to find an open garage door and no vehicles. He was about to dial the second number on the pad when a full-size SUV approached and entered the drive. As he stepped from his truck, he saw the woman do the same. She was in her mid-thirties, reasonably attractive, and massively overdressed for a summer day in rural Mississippi. She carried an expression of curiosity and concern on her face.

Mac introduced himself, and for the second time that day, he saw confusion.

"But I haven't even called you yet. I was just about to."

"I understand. I was at the hospital. I needed to speak to your husband, and they told me you were looking for him."

She absorbed the information before responding. She locked the vehicle with a key fob and stood flat-footed in the drive.

"I don't think he came home last night. I went to work this morning thinking he had just fallen asleep in his office, but when I called later, they told me that he had never shown up for work. I've been trying to call him all day, but he doesn't answer, so I thought I'd better come home."

"Has he ever done this before?"

"No, not like this."

Mac studied her face and saw genuine concern. "So, you would like to file a missing person report?"

She hesitated only momentarily before saying, "Yes, I think I should."

Mac opened his truck door and reached inside for a notepad. "I'll need to contact Seymore PD. It's their jurisdiction. Can we go inside?"

They entered the kitchen from the garage, and she pointed him to a stool in front of a marble countertop. While he made the call, she busied herself by rinsing out the dregs remaining in the pot from the morning coffee and then poured herself a soft drink over ice. She did not offer anything to Mac.

"When did you last see your husband?"

"Yesterday morning, when we both went to work. I have to leave a few minutes before him. I work at the school and have to be there at 7:30. Evan doesn't have to be at the hospital until 8:00."

"Did he seem ok? Was he upset or acting differently? Had there been an argument or an issue between you?" Mac noticed a moment of hesitancy.

"No. No different than usual. He did call about 4:00 yesterday and said he would be working late and not to wait up for him. I went to bed at about 10:00, and then he wasn't here this morning."

"Any friends or family that might know where he is?"

She shook her head. "I called his folks, but they don't know anything. They haven't heard from him all week, and as for friends, his friends are the people he works with."

Mac scanned the neat modern kitchen and the adjoining family room as if looking for something out of place, some clue.

"I apologize for these next questions, but I need to know everything I can. Were the two of you having any marital or financial problems? Were there any mental issues?"

Again, she hesitated, choosing her words carefully. "We're like any married couple. We have our ups and downs, but no, nothing unusual or different, and financially, things have been a lot better recently. Evan's kind of a nervous guy, jumpy, and has a hard time making decisions, but he's always been that way. His work's been stressful lately, that's why we were taking a few days off. We're supposed to go to the Coast this afternoon after work. I've already booked the rooms, lined up some show tickets, and he's taking the kids fishing tomorrow."

"You have children?"

"Yes, two boys. I don't know what to tell them when they get home from school. They were so excited about the trip. I don't know what to do."

Mac looked through the picture window across the adjoining family room and saw a Seymore police cruiser pull into the driveway.

" I'll leave this to the police department, but I recommend you do two things immediately. Check your motel on the Coast; maybe he's there. Maybe there was a miscommunication between the two of you. Then call and make sure your kids are in school."

She stared at him, trying to comprehend the meaning of his last statement.

He rose and said, "There's an officer outside. I'm going out to speak to him and fill him in on what you've told me. Then, I'll put out a missing person report for the county. If you think of anything else, please let us know."

She stood behind the counter, clutching the cold soft drink as he exited the door to the garage.

After briefing the young officer, he returned to the truck and called the office.

"I need to speak to Elam."

Lindon sounded distracted and matter-of-fact. "Can't. He's in the courtroom."

Mac hung up without responding and sent a text.

Possible trouble: Evan Winter is missing. Call when you can.

Mac cranked his truck but then realized he had failed to get a description of Winter's car or a photo. He closed his eyes, took a deep breath, and went back into the house.

***

The next few hours were unproductive. Mac returned to the hospital and spoke with Winter's co-workers. He reviewed his work schedule, and although he had no warrant, he was allowed into the man's office for a cursory look for anything out of place. There was nothing to provide a clue about the man's disappearance.

From the Sheriff's Department briefing room, he had just completed a call to the hotel in Pass Christian that Winter had booked for the weekend when Thompson entered the office. He had obviously not read his text messages.

His eyes widened when he heard of Winter's disappearance. "Well, that's interesting. Maybe we're on the right track, but it does seem odd. Unless there's something else going on in his life we don't know about, why would he run? He didn't know we were going to talk to him. There was nothing to indicate he was a suspect."

Mac said, "You're assuming he's running from something. Like you said, he had no reason to. Maybe there's something else going on."

Thompson's eyes met Mac's, and he knew immediately what he meant. "God, I hope not. Hope he shows up on Monday with his tail between his legs after a long weekend with a chippie down in New Orleans."

"Been known to happen… but I'm not betting on it. What do you say we get with Seymore PD and issue a statewide BOLO for him and his car?"

Thompson said, "Can you handle that? I've got to clear some of this paperwork from court today, and I'm expecting Jimmy back from Hernando at any time now."

Mac nodded. "Have you heard from him? Does he have anything?"

"Damn. I haven't even checked my messages." He pulled out his phone and scrolled through his texts. "Yeah." He paused as he continued to look at the screen. "Should be back in about an hour with a video."

Both men busied themselves. Mac was on the phone with a Seymore police investigator, and Thompson returned to his office, but only after calling for Lindon to make a fresh pot of coffee.

At five thirty, Jimmy Smith strolled into the office in a fine mood, a cased laptop and a manila folder in his hands. He waved Mac in and headed directly for Thompson's office, where he immediately pulled a flash drive from his shirt pocket and handed it to the Sheriff. He looked at Thompson like a kid looked at his Dad after hitting his first home run in little league.

"Not a smoking gun, but it is interesting."

Thompson put the drive into a USB slot in his computer and turned his monitor at an angle so Mac and Smith could huddle around the desk for a view. He found the video file on the drive and opened it.

Almost all security videos are of poor quality; this was no exception: grainy, black, and white. It took a few moments before a black male cloaked in a hoodie placed a boxed cell phone on the counter and reached into his pocket for a wad of bills. The hood hid much of his face, but he was young, without facial hair, and of average build and dress. His mannerisms were relaxed. The clerk pulled a pack of small, flavored cigars from a rack behind him before taking the man's money and he exited the store.

Thompson was disappointed. "That's not much use. Doesn't fit anybody we're looking at. He looks like half the kids in Buford County." He turned to Smith questioningly. "Where's the "almost smoking gun"?"

Jimmy smiled and said, "Hold on - wait for the rest of it."

Almost immediately, the video changed to an outdoor camera, obviously elevated but at some distance from the storefront. The man exited the front doors and walked toward a pair of vehicles. He stopped by the driver's window of a dark-colored F-150. The window rolled down, and a white hand extended to take the phone. The man walked around the truck without exchanging words and entered the car beside it. Within moments, both vehicles exited the parking lot toward the camera, without exposing a license plate. From that distance, the occupants were not visible.

Thompson didn't speak at first, absorbing what he had just seen. "There's our F-150 again, but without tags or a face, it doesn't narrow it down much for us."

Mac nodded in agreement. "It lends credence to our suspicions, but like you said - no smoking gun. There must be a thousand F-150s registered in this county alone."

Jimmy smiled and then said, "424, to be exact. I've been doing my homework. Sheriff, let me sit in your chair for a minute."

Thompson reluctantly rose and made a path for the deputy to sit behind his desk.

Jimmy grabbed the mouse, made a few clicks, and froze the video. "Look, right there." He used the eraser end of a pencil he had grabbed off the desk and almost touched the screen. "Right there."

The frozen image encompassed the truck. "You see this right in front of the F-150 on the side. I know it's not plain, but there's nothing else it could be."

Mac was the first to recognize it. "King Ranch"

"Yep, King Ranch and there ain't many of those in this county."

CHAPTER 29

It had been raining heavily since midnight. The storm had moved slowly and now had reached a near standstill, releasing its bowels atop Buford County. The lightning and thunder that had announced its approach dissipated during the night, leaving a heavy downpour that eventually slowed to a steady drizzle as daylight broke. Bouts of rain and dreary skies were expected throughout the remainder of the weekend.

Mac rose to the smell of coffee and bacon. He groaned and stretched to loosen his joints before dressing in yesterday's clothes and heading to the kitchen. Mary was already dressed for the outside world except for a pair of tattered house slippers.

She poured his coffee while he helped himself to the bacon and eggs on the stove before kissing her on the cheek. There was no conversation between them as they ate and then placed the soiled dishes in the dishwasher.

They stood silently for a moment, drinking the last of the coffee before Mac said, "Ready?"

Mary nodded before removing rain gear from a peg in the mudroom and slipping on the rubber boots she usually used in the garden. Mac grabbed an umbrella from the old milk can by the door and followed her into the soft rain.

The county supervisor had family buried in the cemetery, and the gravel road was well maintained, but Mac had to stop in the roadway once to remove a limb that had fallen in last night's storm. The narrow road was shielded from the light drizzle by the canopy of trees, but heavy drops fell all around him, bombarding him and the truck. Drops had accumulated on the tops of leaves until they combined too heavily and fell like liquid glass. He brushed the moisture from his head with his hand and smiled at Mary when he re-entered the truck and drove forward.

The graveyard seemed a lonely place to some. There was no adjoining church and no houses along the way. The road only served the cemetery, cut through deep woods surrounding a three-acre clearing that served as a home for five generations of family dead.

They entered the rusty gate in the chain link fence and walked through the heavy mist to a marker near the back of the cemetery. Mary pulled the wilted flowers from a glass vase in front of a modern headstone and handed them to Mac. He walked to the graveyard's edge and tossed them over the fence while she placed fresh carnations and firmed the vase in the soft ground.

"They didn't hold up too well in last week's heat, did they?"

She didn't respond, not wanting to acknowledge the futility of fresh flowers in a graveyard in the Mississippi heat, but simply backed away and stood by his side at the foot of the grave. Minutes passed as they stood in silence, lost in their own memories and sadness.

Mac finally spoke and nodded toward the empty plots beside the marker. "I suppose there is a comfort knowing where you will be buried."

Her eyes never left the marker. "I take greater comfort in knowing where I'll spend eternity."

Throughout their marriage and their loss, Mac marveled at her faith and continually questioned his own. He usually felt that his belief was solid, but there were times when he felt his convictions weaken; an abused child, the hypocrisy of a church member, or events like those of the last few weeks raised questions and doubts that were hard to resolve.

"You come here by yourself sometimes." A statement, not a question.

"Sometimes. I just need to talk to him. I find some comfort in it."

He found her hand, now wet from the moisture that slipped from the cuff of her rain jacket, and bowed his head.

"Dear God, Thank you for the time we were allowed with this young man............"

CHAPTER 30

It was a lazy Sunday afternoon. The storm had passed. The rain had stopped entirely by midmorning, but the last of the cloud cover remained, tamping down the heat and softening the humidity. Elam Thompson had just finished a short nap after a Sunday dinner. He was now sweeping out his garage and picking up debris that had blown across his yard during the weather.

By noon, the runoff had cleared the shallow ditch that ran across his backyard, making its way down the hills and through the woods into the small creek at the base of his property. Other than a few puddles in low, shaded spots and wallowed ruts in rural roads and paths, any sign of the weekend's downpour would be gone by Monday morning.

As he bent to pick up a small pine limb, he saw Caroline turn the corner of the house, his cell phone in her hand. She held it high above her head as if it were distasteful, a look of disgust on her face. She walked across the yard, handed him the phone, and turned back to the house without comment.

He watched her walk away, a sense of guilt and regret that grew with each passing year stirring inside of him.

"Yeah."

He was silent as he listened. Jimmy Smith was the deputy on duty for the weekend.

"I know where it is. Are you on your way?"

Another pause, and then he said, "I'll be about thirty minutes, and Jimmy, don't touch anything. Bring your camera, and before you drive in, look for any tire tracks. With all this rain, we could get lucky."

He disconnected the call and placed another. "Mac, sorry to call you on Sunday, but we may have found our pharmacist."

***

Mac had some difficulty finding the turnoff into the deer camp and was a full twenty minutes behind Thompson. He drove into the clearing to find two department vehicles parked near a dark maroon sedan and an older Dodge pickup by the leaning hulk of a cabin.

Thompson didn't bother to introduce the older man in overalls and t-shirt. The man was obviously shaken, his hands inside the bib and his eyes wide, a toothpick stuck in the corner of his mouth.

"OK, tell us again now that Mac's here, and I'll let you get out of here. I know it's a shock to you."

He drew Mac closer, and he saw the body in the driver's seat of the sedan for the first time. The driver's side window had obviously been down during the weekend rain. As a result, much of the interior and Winter's clothes and hair were soaked.

"Like I said, I drove in about one o'clock after I ate dinner. I check the place every Sunday, especially today, cause I wanted to see if we had any storm damage. I saw the car, and at first, thought somebody was sleeping one off, but as soon as I took a good look at him, I knew he was dead, the window down and all wet inside. I went back to the house and called 911."

"And you didn't see anyone else?"

"No, sir. Don't see many folks out this way unless they belong here."

Mac said, "What about Friday – or maybe Thursday evening?"

The man shook his head. "I drive a truck during the week. I didn't get home until late Friday—just before the rain started."

"Did you see any tire tracks when you came in?"

"Can't say I was looking, but I don't think so."

Thompson placed his hand on the man's shoulder and said, "The rain would have washed any tracks away unless they were made today. One more thing. We believe this man is a fellow named Evan Winter. He wouldn't be a member of your club, would he?"

"Naw, I ain't never seen him before – at least I don't think so. But a man don't look the same when he's dead." He rolled the toothpick from one side of his mouth to the other.

"We're just a bunch of good ol' boys and a few rednecks. We play cards, drink a little, and shoot a few deer." He stared at the dead man in the car. "He don't look like a good ol' boy."

As the man drove out of the clearing, Thompson turned to Mac, standing by the sedan. "So, you think Thursday night, too?"

"It had to be. The rain would have washed away any tracks, and the inside of that car is soaked."

Thompson looked at his phone. "I'm going to have to go back to the road and maybe a little further. Can't get a signal in here. Ya'll do what you do, and I'll be back."

Mac directed Jimmy to take more photos of the car and close-ups of the body through the window. Winter's face was drained of color, his hair plastered to his head. Both men slipped on gloves and began to dig further. There was no sign of blood or tissue damage, nothing to indicate how the man died. Mac pulled a pencil from his pocket and used it to raise the man's upper lip, exposing near-perfect teeth. Then, he used it to explore the pocket of the man's white Oxford shirt while Jimmy walked to the passenger side of the car.

"Looks like he's holding something in his right hand."

"Yep. Looks like a pill bottle." He looked across the top of the car at Jimmy. "There's an envelope on the seat. It's soaked. Grab a couple of evidence baggies."

"What are you thinking – a suicide?"

"Could be." Mac stared into the dead face, looking for answers. "It could be, but I bet it ain't."

***

It was rare to see lights burning bright in the courthouse basement on a Sunday night. It drew the attention of the few locals who drove through the square on their way home from Sunday night church services or across town to the fast-food joints for ice cream and milkshakes. Lacking more diverse forms of entertainment, speculation and rumors about the purpose would spread around coffee clutches, offices, and breakrooms on Monday morning.

Dolan had now joined Thompson, Mac, and Jimmy Smith as they sat around a conference table. A small pill bottle and a note, recently removed from the envelope and slowly allowed to dry, lined the table in front of Thompson. With gloved hands and a pair of cosmetic tweezers, he unfolded the note and read it aloud. On separate lines in a computer font were the following:

I'm Sorry

I did it

Forgive me

Thompson looked at the faces around him and waited for comments.

Dolan was the first to speak. "Just what exactly did he do?

Thompson didn't respond but stared at Mac, waiting for the investigator to provide something of substance.

"Well, it could be a suicide but I don't buy it." Mac pushed back his chair slightly and crossed his legs. "Contrary to what you see in movies and cheap novels, most suicides don't leave a note ... especially not one like this."

"What do you mean?" This was Jimmy Smith's first serious investigation since joining the department, and he was now engrossed.

Mac said, "A suicide note is personal, the most personal thing a man will ever write. A man wants to explain himself, ask for forgiveness, or extract revenge from someone who wronged him. Why was it typed? Why was it so vague? Why did he bother to put it in an envelope?"

He paused momentarily to make sure his remarks were properly understood. "You might type a note if you're going to do away with yourself in an office or maybe even at home but out in the middle of nowhere? It's more likely he would write it by hand on whatever was available. Just doesn't fit. None of this fits. From what I've learned of the man, he was a scared rabbit, and scared rabbits don't commit suicide. They might have a mental breakdown, confess like a blathering fool, or run for the hills, but they don't kill themselves."

Thompson recalled Doc Barton's description of Winter – *"scared rabbit"*. He was convinced but didn't comment, waiting for further discussion from those around the table. He picked up the pill bottle and examined it. There was no label and he removed the cap. Inside were half a dozen round yellow pills.

"Valium- diazepam."

He shook the bottle and started to pour the pills into his hand.

"Wait!" Mac spoke loudly and harshly, waving his hands.

Thompson froze and turned the bottle upright. "What the hell?"

"You had better get some help taking off those gloves - just to be safe."

Thompson's confusion cleared as he realized his near mistake. He held his hands above the table and away from his body. "I didn't touch any of them…. I don't think."

Dolan was puzzled and slightly unnerved. "I don't understand. They're just pills."

Mac rose, donned gloves from a box on the nearby counter, and carefully helped the Sheriff remove his, rolling them inside out and placing them on the table.

Mac looked at Dolan. "Think about it. If Winters was going to kill himself with those pills, why didn't he take all of them?"

Jimmy Smith's eyes brightened. "Fentanyl."

***

Monday morning started early, and by seven thirty, even Dolan had arrived with a bag full of breakfast biscuits in his hand.

Thompson held a quick meeting and delegated responsibilities. He'd made a decision to keep Jimmy Smith on the investigation on a full-time basis.

Smith began sorting through the list of King Ranch trucks with model years 2021 or 2022 while Dolan inventoried evidence from the deer camp. Thompson was not yet prepared to call it a crime scene, but he planned to treat it as one.

Mac would assist Thompson in compiling and organizing the details needed for an eleven o'clock meeting with the district attorney in hopes of obtaining warrants, not only for the free clinic and pharmacies, but they would also try for the hospital pharmacy records and maybe Winter's financial records. Even if the man's death were ruled a suicide, there would be questions that needed answers.

While Mac made notes, Thompson dialed the state coroner's office in Jackson. After waiting on hold and enduring several conversations with receptionists and low-level bureaucrats, he finally was connected with an assistant coroner familiar with his cases.

"We suspect fentanyl. That's the first thing to look for." He listened for a moment and shook his head at Mac. "I know you're backed up, but just to let you know, we think this death may be connected to two others we sent you last week. We're pushing for warrants and need whatever you can give us."

When Thompson hung up the phone, he looked at Mac and grimaced. "We're low man on the totem pole. Not a lot of political power coming from little ol' Buford County. Do you know what he told me? Said – to hold my damned britches, they'd get to me when they get to me."

Mac knew that the state crime lab and coroner's office were understaffed, underfunded and like every state agency in Mississippi, politics and power pushed the pedal. It had been a source of irritation and discussion for local law enforcement for decades.

"I don't suppose the local coroner could be much help?"

"No, none at all. He's a good man, but he's a retired funeral director and has no medical knowledge at all. His job is mainly documenting nursing home deaths and traffic accidents."

Thompson needed to organize his thoughts and reconsider his tactics. The cases had come quickly, and up until this point, he had simply reacted to the events and evidence that surfaced. "Let's lay this out, just like I need to present it to the DA and a judge."

Mac grabbed a legal pad in his lap and began to compile notes as he spoke. "We've got the homicides of two young men with similar backgrounds, killed in a similar manner but no ballistics yet. Both had a significant quantity of prescription drugs. At least one passed forged prescriptions that likely came from the local free clinic."

Thompson nodded in agreement. "And we've got some cell phone evidence that connects the two just before each homicide. That burner phone was purchased at a truck stop in North Mississippi a few weeks before their deaths. A dark-colored King Ranch F-150 was identified at the purchase, and a dark F-150 was seen near the scene of one of the crimes: a truck we can't tie to anyone."

Mac then added, "The quantity of drugs involved would indicate that there was another source. I believe the prescriptions were just a way to supplement the supply, and that's how our victims got involved. That amount of drugs would have to be coming from a major local supply like a pharmacy. So now we've got a suspicious death of a hospital pharmacist and a possible suicide note that may or may not implicate him."

Thompson pulled a cigarette from the pack in his pocket and stuck it in his mouth before realizing he couldn't light it. "There's too many "may or may nots" in this case."

Mac said, "I don't believe it was a suicide, but whoever killed Winter did us a favor with that note."

Thompson looked at him curiously.

"The note is a direct implication that Winter was involved in something illegal or, at best, unethical. Given the circumstances, that should be sufficient for a warrant of the pharmacy records and his financials."

Thompson silently agreed as Mac continued to make notes. "Do you think there's any chance that Winter is our shooter- maybe couldn't live with the guilt? I mean, that would wrap things up nice and tidy."

"No way. Winter was a local boy; the hospital had employed him for almost ten years, and by all accounts, he was not the type. No, I think someone pulled him into this, and he got in over his head."

"You're thinking Louis Rich, aren't you?"

Mac was about to respond when Jimmy appeared in the doorway. "I got a breakdown on those F-150's, Boss."

"OK, let's have it. The DA will be here any time now."

Jimmy read from his pad. "Forty-eight King Ranch's registered in the county. Twenty-two of them are model years 2021 and 2022. Fourteen of those are black, light gray, or what they call metallic gray. Four of those are registered to Seymore Manufacturing. I think they provide them to their salesmen. Of the ten remaining, two belong to a couple of old landowners who have more money than God. I don't think they would be high on the suspect list. Six belong to folks I don't know, but I'll track them down."

Thompson looked at Jimmy expectantly. He already knew the answer but wanted the young deputy to have the pleasure of telling them. "That leaves two and who do they belong to?"

"Ed Lang and Louis Rich."

CHAPTER 31

Fugly Brown was a torn man. He'd gambled once with Louis Rich. He wasn't sure he was prepared to do it again. He had spent a restless night, rising twice to watch his young son sleeping in a bassinet beside the bed. Fugly finally gave up any attempts at sleep and sat on the couch playing with the Xbox till the sun began to rise, his mind racing.

His court-appointed attorney said that he could be out in twelve to fifteen months with good behavior. He could do that. Maybe the girl and the boy would still be there. It's not like she had anywhere to go or a lot of options.

He had two choices: Stay on Rich and hit him up for more money or tell the Sheriff what he knew and maybe get his time cut even more. That could possibly expose his extortion of Rich. He realized he had a third choice – to do nothing. There was no risk in that, but then again, there was no benefit either.

The girl grunted at him as she entered the room. Clad in an old t-shirt and light pajama bottoms emblazoned with cartoon characters, she opened the refrigerator door and asked, "Help me warm up a bottle?"

***

Louis Rich glared as he saw Fugly enter the waiting area of the free clinic. He avoided any other eye contact as he busied himself with patients. It was ten o'clock before he called Fugly back to an exam room.

Fugly jumped up on the exam table, false arrogance in his attitude. Rich did not speak but simply stared at the man. He knew what he wanted.

"I've been doing some calculations, Doc. What with this inflation and all, I don't think five grand is gonna do it for me. Have you seen what diapers cost nowadays?"

Rich's lack of response and cold stare set Fugly on edge, and he kept talking, hoping it would calm his nerves. "I need another five grand. That'll be the end of it, I promise."

Rich walked further into the room, pulled out a plastic chair, and sat, leaning forward, his forearms on his knees. "That's what you said last time."

"I know, I know, and I meant it, but we had some emergency expenditures. You know how it is, but then again, maybe you don't. The girl was behind on some car payments. She can't get to work without her car."

"I am not a man you want to mess with, boy." Rich rose as he spoke, his eyes on fire, and for a moment, Fugly feared that he might strike him. He pulled back slightly and betrayed any pretense of control he thought he might have in the situation.

But Rich only continued to stare. "I don't have another five. I could maybe get you one, maybe two grand, but that's it."

For the first time, Fugly feared the man. He had not been convinced that Rich had killed Dean and Deeter before, but now, he was sure. He decided not to push it any further.

"I'm not unreasonable, Doc. I know you'll do what you can."

"It'll be a while. I can't just pull that kind of money out of my accounts. If they do get suspicious and check my bank records, I'll have to explain it, and that won't be good for me or you."

Fugly nodded as if he understood even though he had little comprehension of bank accounts or financial record keeping.

"Well, you could just tell them you lost it in the casino. It's not like that doesn't happen every day around here. Hell, that's just folding money for a man like you."

Rich ignored the response. "Next Thursday, I'll see what I can do, but that's the last of it." He repeated it slowly and in a level tone. "That is the absolute last of it."

Fugly nodded again and smiled in agreement. "Absolutely. Besides, you won't have to worry about me much longer. I'm headed to Parchman in less than six weeks. That money sure will ease my mind while I'm gone."

"One last thing." Rich walked toward the exam room door and grabbed the handle. "Don't come back here. Cops are nosing around, and they asked specifically about you."

Fugly feigned surprise and put his hand on his chest before laughing. "Yeah, they've already questioned me. I knew them boys pretty well. You had to know they'd wanna talk to me. But don't worry, your name never came up."

He scratched his head and said, "Alright, not here, but it's gonna have to be in a public place. My life ain't much, but it's mine. I already got it figured out. You get off here around one o'clock? Be at Delmer's convenience store on the edge of town at 1:15. I'll be pumping gas. You come by to fill up and park next to me if you can. Just toss the money envelope in my car window as you walk by." He grinned. "I'll be sure the window's down."

"Convenience stores have security cameras – that's no good."

"Don't worry, Doc. That place is my second home. I know everything about it and them security cameras…… They ain't worked in two years."

***

Louis Rich had driven by the Southgate apartments three times in the last week. One evening, he had even pulled into the parking area and parked his car beside an old van with two flat tires, a van that had obviously not been moved in months. Rich watched until his presence attracted too much interest from barefoot kids and loose dogs. He knew which apartment belonged to Fugly and his girlfriend, and he knew that Fugly was almost always there. Given the traffic at the complex, the fact that folks sat outside in the evenings on the porches, and the lack of any cover, he knew there was no way to get at him. Rich thought Fugly was an ignorant redneck, but he was either damned careful or damned lucky.

He had reached an unsatisfying decision. Fugly Brown was outside of his reach.

He turned his car toward north Seymore and entered a subdivision. He stopped at the intersection long enough to observe the driveway of Evan Winter's home, making sure there were no visitors or law enforcement present before parking in front of the garage.

He was met at the door by Lucy Winter. "You probably shouldn't be here, Louis."

"I just came by to offer my condolences. It would look odd if I didn't. Are you ok? Where are the kids?"

She walked in front of him into the house. "I'm starting to get a grip. The kids are at Evan's folks. We thought it would be better for them there." She sat down in an oversized lounger and curled her legs underneath her.

"There's just too much stuff I don't understand. Evan wasn't the kind of man to kill himself. He – He was too much of a coward." Her voice trailed off as she absorbed the bitterness of her last words. She crossed her arms and ran her hands up each shoulder as if to comfort herself.

"You never know what's in somebody else's mind, Lucy." He sat on the sofa across from her, waiting for her to say more.

"The Sheriff's Department was here earlier. They had a lot of questions. I don't think they're convinced it was suicide. They didn't say anything, but I just got that feeling. Kept asking about financial stuff and his work."

"Well, what did you tell them?"

"What could I tell them? We kept separate bank accounts, and he paid all the bills. I'm not even sure how much he made every month. I just know we weren't behind on any bills, and he had a 401k."

"Did he have life insurance?"

For the first time, he saw tears.

"Not much, just a policy through work – fifty thousand, I think. That won't even pay off the house. That's another reason…" She hesitated and veered away from the thought. "I kept telling him we needed more insurance, but he wouldn't do it - always made an excuse. I think it scared him – reminded him of his own mortality."

Rich's only response was a nod and a sorrowful expression.

She watched him closely and wavered in her thoughts before saying, "I'm glad you're here, despite what I said before. I just gotta talk to someone about this."

His eyes followed her as she rose from the chair, walked to the kitchen, and pulled something from an overhead cabinet. As she returned to the lounger, she dropped a wad of bills wrapped in a rubber band on the coffee table.

"After the cops came here asking about money, I got curious. I found that in a shoebox in our closet. There's almost twenty thousand in there. I don't know where it came from."

Rich whistled and picked up the wad. "He never told you about it?"

She shook her head. "I'm beginning to think that maybe he was involved in something at work."

"Like what?"

"I dunno. He was a pharmacist. It'd have to be drugs."

"What are you going to do, Lucy?" he pointed at the money on the table.

"I don't know." She looked him directly in the eye. "I need some advice."

He held the clump of bills in his hand and studied it, feeling its weight. "Based on what you just told me, you'll need this money. I don't think you should tell anyone."

"That's what I was thinking, too. I'm just so confused. I can't believe he put me in this situation."

He stood up and handed her the bills, staring at the top of her head. "You asked for advice, so here it is. If Evan was involved in something illegal at the hospital, it will come out, and that means they'd look at all your finances and purchases. They'll also search this house. You need to find somewhere or someone to keep it until this is all over. Do you have anyone you trust—outside of the family, I mean?"

She didn't hesitate. "No, I don't want to draw anyone else into this. Folks around here live on rumors. It's bad enough that your husband commits suicide, but if he was a criminal as well…."

Her voice softened as she looked up at him. In a pleading tone, she said, "Will you hold it for me?"

He smiled and touched her shoulder. "Sure, Lucy. I'll hold it for you. It'll be there when you need it."

She handed him the bills, and he tucked them inside his pants pocket.

"I don't think he knew about us, do you?" She looked at him plaintively.

"No. He'd have freaked if he did. He couldn't hide that from me or you, for that matter. He didn't know. Besides, that was in the past."

She was silent for a while. Depression and fear had replaced the shock. Lucy finally reached across the coffee table and took his hand. She spoke in a near whisper. "I know it's terrible of me, but I don't have many friends in this town. I don't want to be alone. Would you stay with me tonight – at least for a while?"

For the first time, he felt discomfort and struggled to find the right words: "Lucy, there's nothing I would like better, but I don't think so. You said it yourself. You don't need rumors. It wouldn't look right, and you never know who's going to come to the door; a little ol' blue-haired lady with a casserole or a pot of chicken and dumplings. Don't forget where we are. They feed the bereaved around here."

CHAPTER 32

By mid-summer, the oppressive heat slowed life around Seymore and Buford County. The last vacation bible school had been completed, and parents were planning vacations and weekend trips to lakes and theme parks before schools opened their doors in August. Those who weren't preoccupied with such things found the slower pace ideal for firing up a rumor mill that kept pumping out an endless assortment of tales. The most prevalent was that an urban gang with roots in New Orleans had infiltrated their sleepy little town and was the source of all drugs, death, and potential destruction on their doorsteps.

As a result, the Buford County Sheriff's Department and the police forces of Seymore and Coyville saw a marked increase in 911 calls about strange vehicles and unknown outsiders.

A doomed salesman offering burial insurance door-to-door in the northern region of the county was questioned five times by Thompson's deputies before packing his bags and heading to friendlier territory.

Elam Thompson's mood was not enhanced by the extra workload created by the local hysteria nor by his recent doctor's appointment that would inevitably lead to more upcoming appointments, and he now had to remember to take pills for the first time in his life – probably for the rest of his life.

As with any crime that was not solved quickly, his investigation settled onto a long trail of endless paperwork, false leads, and frustration. It would be the next Friday before he held the final autopsies and crime lab reports of Jason Deeter, Jason Dean, and Evan Winter in his hand. As he settled into his office chair, he found little value or satisfaction in their content.

Ballistics showed that Dean and Deeter had "probably" been killed with the same gun, a twenty-two automatic using subsonic hollow point ammunition. Deeter's toxicology report came back clean, and Dean only had marijuana in his system at the time of death.

Evan Winter's paperwork was even less satisfying. Thompson took more time to fully read and absorb the medical examiner's report:

Fully developed white male, aged 36 years, height – 5'10" weight – 195 lbs. Brown hair of medium length.

Clothed with no visible injuries or blood loss. No tattoos or significant scarring

Time of death – at least 48 hours prior to time of discovery

Cause of death indicated as pulmonary edema caused by fentanyl poisoning

Manner of death – undetermined. The nature of death could not rule out homicide, suicide or accident.

The reports had been exactly as he suspected and offered no new evidence or surprises that might move the cases forward.

By nine o'clock, Thompson had pulled Dolan and Mac into the conference room and provided each of them with copies of the reports. He poured a cup of coffee while giving them a few moments to review the information. "Where do we go from here?"

"Still no warrants?" asked Mac.

Thompson shook his head. "It's in the hands of the DA now. I think we'll get them, but you know that the bureaucracy moves slowly."

Dolan rubbed the side of his face, moving his fingers over the bristle of a new beard he had started the week before. "Without warrants, I suppose all we can do is try to trace the gun – not that there's much to go on."

Mac agreed. "While it's not likely, I think we should check if any firearms are registered to Evan Winter and Louis Rich…. And just for kicks, let's throw in Ed Lang."

Thompson was pessimistic. He knew that most handguns in Mississippi were not registered and that this killer was not stupid enough to use a traceable weapon. "Yeah, not likely, but what the hell. Let's include Arlene Deeter and Winter's and Lang's spouses as well."

Thompson thought of the pile of cases on his desk; petty thefts, one runaway teenager, warrants for domestic abuse and assault. He was tired, and the flood of information scattered his thoughts. "Gentlemen, we're just spinning our wheels here without those warrants. Dolan, have Jimmy check out the firearm registry. You can go back to clearing some of the cases on your desk for the rest of the day. We'll take the weekend to clear our heads and get a fresh start on Monday."

As Dolan left the room, Thompson drained his coffee and looked at Mac. "I got a strange one cooking down on Flat Line Road. You wanna tag along?"

*****

The day-to-day existence of a rural law enforcement officer is diverse, sometimes bizarre, and always frustrating. A sheriff or an investigator will exit the scene of a traffic accident or a bloody homicide to calm a domestic disturbance, pull an abused child from the arms of a twisted parent, or separate neighbors bloodying each other over a hunting lease. To survive, a man has to find humor when he can and not peer below the surface of things when they get too grim.

Elam had piqued Mac's interest, and it was too hot to fish or do garden work, so he took to the passenger seat of the Sheriff's truck and enjoyed the air-conditioned ride to the call a few miles south of town. Given the pile of cases on the Sheriff's desk, he thought it was strange that he would respond personally to a simple vandalism case, but Thompson seemed intrigued.

Flat Line Road ran in a southeasterly direction, parallel to a twisting sand creek that barely flowed in the summer but raged in the winter months. The two-lane blacktop was lined with small FHA homes, a few old homesteads, and doublewides.

"Fella's name is Taggert. Called in this morning, madder n hell, but I couldn't make much sense out of what he was saying." Thompson pointed ahead to a rusted mailbox with faded lettering – 4117. He pulled the truck into the drive and passed a small clump of trees in the front yard. A man dressed in a t-shirt and shorts was leaning against the trunk of a white Toyota. He straightened, folded his arms, and shook his head as the men approached.

Mac surveyed the yard and home for signs of vandalism but saw nothing out of the ordinary. The house was small but neat, with a half-brick front, and it appeared to be well-maintained.

"Mr. Taggert, I'm Sheriff Thompson, and this is Bill McKenzie. What's going on here?"

"Well, isn't it obvious?' The man pointed at the house.

The two men looked at each other, but neither comprehended the problem.

Sensing their confusion, the man's frustration took over. "Come here, let me show you. It's as plain as the nose on your face." He violently waved them toward the house near the edge of the carport before pointing at the blue lapboard that started at waist height. "Right there!"

After a moment of silence, Thompson said, "I'm sorry, Mr. Taggert. I guess we're just not getting it. Maybe you better start at the beginning."

The man started to speak and then halted, trying to calm himself. "Ok…Ok. My wife and I went to Tupelo yesterday for a doctor's appointment. We left early because her appointment was at nine o'clock, and we decided to make a day of it. We went out to eat, did some shopping, and decided to spend the night. When we got home this morning, we found this." Again, he pointed at the lapboard.

"Uh-huh," Thompson looked at the man, still confused.

"It's blue, man, it's blue!"

Both men repeated, "Uh -huh."

Taggert shook his fist. "It's supposed to be white."

Mac was the first to speak. "You mean you called the Sheriff's office because your painter used the wrong paint?"

"It ain't just the wrong paint. I didn't contract with anybody to paint my house. It was just painted two years ago. Best I can figure some sumbitch painted the wrong house!"

The drive back to town served to ease the tension that had been building over the last few weeks. Mac laughed. "I'm still not sure you convinced him that it's a civil matter. He wasn't too happy with you."

"Yeah, probably lost a vote on that one. I've heard of that- a contractor painting the wrong house, but I've never seen it."

"I guess… if you want…. I could check the hardware stores and see who bought blue paint lately."

"Munchkin."

"What?"

"Munchkin Brown, only painter I know that could screw up that bad. Come to think of it, I believe he's Fugly's uncle."

Mac laughed. "In small town Mississippi, it ain't six degrees of separation. It's only bout two."

"What's that?"

He just shook his head. "Nothin'."

***

Louis Rich hadn't shown up. Fugly had waited at Delmer's for ten minutes, pulled away to avoid suspicion, and parked down the street in a discount store parking lot with a view of the gas pumps. He returned five minutes later and took his time pumping ten dollars of gas into the girl's car. He made a point of explaining to the clerk that he had forgotten his wallet when he was there earlier. The kid behind the counter showed no interest and simply grunted at him.

Fugly drove to the clinic and found it closed. He then drove to the east side of town and searched for Rich's truck in the hospital employee parking lot without success. He considered going inside and asking for the man but judged against it.

He spent the next few days in a state of near rage. He felt that he was never going to see that money. His mind was tossed between the fear that Rich had skipped town and the rationalization that a man like that couldn't just pick up and leave overnight. He had too many attachments: a job, a lease, furniture, and obligations.

Sitting on the couch, babysitting the child, he googled Louis Rich in Seymore, Mississippi, hoping to find an address. No luck. He expanded the search to include the entire state. A line of names popped up, and he did a social media search of the most likely candidates. After an hour of viewing pictures of family men with their kids, fishing and golf buddies, truck drivers, and teenagers in rock band t-shirts, he expanded the search again to include Tennessee.

After ten minutes, he found a likely candidate with an address in Bartlett, Tennessee. Only a street address and no social accounts. He pulled up Google Maps, typed in the address, and switched to Street View. The image showed an area of vacant lots with a row of conventional houses in the distant background. He checked the date on the photography and found that it was two years old.

He knew there had to be some online record of the man: a utility bill, insurance, a car registration, something, but he realized he lacked the skills and patience to have much success.

He placed the phone on the cheap glass coffee table and picked up a controller for his Xbox.

Monday morning- free clinic, and there would be hell to pay.

CHAPTER 33

Elam Thompson was refreshed, hopeful for the first time in weeks. An uninterrupted weekend had provided the opportunity to rest and clear his head. Time with his wife around the kitchen table had resulted in some planned changes to his diet, and he had begun to accept that barbeque, fast-food burgers, and mashed potatoes would not be a significant part of his life moving forward. He skipped the sausage biscuit that morning in lieu of scrambled eggs.

Lindon stopped him as he entered the office. "Mornin', Boss. Those warrants came in. They're on your desk, and you have someone waiting in the conference room."

After grabbing coffee, Thompson found Denise Mayfair sitting in a chair against the wall, holding a small brown paper bag. "Good morning. How are you doing?"

"I'm ok, Sheriff. I want to thank you for the help with the funeral homes. They released Jason's body last week. He's going to be cremated in Jackson, and we'll have a private service here later."

"Well, I'm glad you were able to work it out." He sat down beside her. "I am sorry for your loss. Bad circumstances, I know. I wish I had more to tell you about his case. We are making progress, but I really can't say much right now."

"I understand. I've been around enough to know that when drugs are involved…. things get complicated."

"Yes, ma'am."

"That's why I'm here. Jason still kept a few things at my house. I started going through his stuff, and I found this in a box under some video games and computer cables." She pulled a small pad from the bag and handed it to Thompson.

"He wasn't supposed to have that, was he?"

The watermark "Buford Medical Trust" was plainly visible. He shuffled through the pad and found only half a dozen sheets remaining of what had obviously been a much larger pad. "No, ma'am, he wasn't supposed to have that."

"Will that help?"

"It just might, It just might." He looked at the woman dressed in a hospital smock and sensible shoes, a degree of hopefulness on her face. "Any chance you would have something with Jason's handwriting on it?"

***

The warrants were waiting for him when he reached his desk; one for the work and prescription records at the Buford Medical Clinic and one for the pharmacy inventory and accounting at the hospital. The warrant covered everything from last Friday back for a period of one year. Thompson knew a political bombshell when he saw it. He had to be careful how he approached this. Fortunately, the same local attorney represented the hospital and the clinic. It was a small town.

"We meeting this morning, Sheriff?" Jimmy Smith stood in the doorway.

"Yep, get everybody together, and I'll be right there." He picked up the warrants and the prescription pad and walked across the hallway.

"Mac and I will deliver the warrants to the attorney this morning." He slid them across the table after Jimmy had made copies for all of them. "We'll have to handle this discreetly, especially the hospital. Too much bad press of any kind can kill a little hospital. I'll go over this afternoon and talk to Ed Lang. Give him a heads-up and a chance to make copies of any records. Is anybody good with financials?"

No one responded.

"Yeah, I didn't think so."

Mac said, "I know a guy in Jackson. JPD used him on a few cases, and I think he specializes in hospital and nursing home audits, but…" He paused and looked across the table at Thompson. "You'll have to pay him."

"Got any idea what that would cost?"

"A hospital audit can cost fifteen to twenty thousand, so I think maybe half of that. He's a good guy. He might take pity on you."

Thompson considered this; his mind was absorbed by a department budget that was already a hundred thousand in the hole for the year. "Let's wait until we get the records, and then we'll decide."

He reached into his shirt pocket and tossed the prescription pad on the table. "That was in Jason Dean's possession."

Dolan and Smith leaned forward in their chairs to get a closer look.

Mac didn't react. He knew what the pad was and where it came from. "Well, that's a winner, ain't it?"

"It does show that we're on the right track, but I don't want to be too single-minded here. It's easy to get lost on a rabbit trail when you should be looking for a fox. Have we excluded any other possibilities? Could these drugs be coming from some other source than the clinic or the hospital?"

Smith eyed the Sheriff. "I don't think so. Everything points in that direction."

Dolan spoke. "I don't think it's likely, but what about that Doc out near the highway – that foreign fella. Lots of folks don't like him. Can't really say why, but there have been a few rumors circulating since he got here."

Thompson frowned. "I've heard those rumors, too, but Etau's not our man. The only reason some folks don't like him is cause of what you just said – he's a foreign fellow. He treats black folks almost exclusively, and instead of a lawn, he's got a pile of sand and a pair of fake palm trees in his backyard. Folks don't like different."

Mac agreed but wondered at the forcefulness of the Elam's opinion. "No, I think Jimmy's right. We're chasing the right fox."

Jimmy Smith beamed. "I got something else. I got that firearm information. He pulled a folder from his lap and set it on the table. "Nothing registered to Deeter, Rich, Lang, or his wife or Evan Winter, but there is a Ruger SR22 registered to one Ms. Lucy Denise Winter.

***

Lucy Winter was drained, weary of her circumstances, and worried about what the future would bring. She'd spent the morning at the funeral home making arrangements with Evan's father. She had no idea that a service could be so expensive, but at least the payment would be deferred until Evan's insurance check arrived.

The body was scheduled for return on Tuesday, and the funeral was planned for 2:30 on Wednesday. Evan would be buried in his family's church cemetery, and a meal would be served afterward. She dreaded the hugs from people she hardly knew, the downward, sorrowful expressions, and the questions she couldn't answer. She just wanted it all to be over.

She felt that she had abandoned her kids, leaving them in the care of Evan's parents, but she couldn't deal with all the emotions and tears. She believed that his parents blamed her for Evan's death. There had been long periods of silence, stares from across the room, and delicate but pointed questions.

She needed a friend. Calls to Louis Rich's cell phone had gone straight to voicemail, and her best friend lived two states away and was vacationing in Bermuda. She never felt more alone in her life.

She sat on the sofa, sipping a diet soda over crushed ice, with Evan's checkbook, bank statements, and a copy of the insurance policy on the table before her. As she crunched on the remaining ice, she saw two Sheriff's Department vehicles pull into the drive.

She met them at the door and opened it before they rang the bell.

"Ms. Winter, do you mind if we come in?"

She pushed the door back further and motioned them in. "Do you have some more information?"

Mac said, "Yes, ma'am, and we have a few more questions. Could we sit down?"

She led them into the family room, took a seat, and poured the remainder of the soda into her glass.

"This is Sheriff Thompson. He can update you on what we have."

Thompson sat stiffly in a chair. "I am sorry for your loss. I hope your kids are ok."

She said, "As well as can be expected. They're young enough that they don't understand it all. They're at Evan's parents."

"Yes, ma'am. We've got the autopsy report back on your husband. He died of fentanyl poisoning. He went quickly. Unfortunately, the coroner could not determine if it was suicide or something else."

She didn't respond at first as Mac watched closely, observing her body language and facial expressions.

"Something else – meaning what?"

"An accidental overdose, or perhaps someone did this to him."

She shook her head. "Evan didn't take drugs. He twisted his knee last year, and he kept a bottle of painkillers in the cabinet, but he rarely ever took one. He knew the danger involved. You said fentanyl. Evan wouldn't knowingly take fentanyl. Isn't that a street drug?"

Mac responded. "Yes and no. Dealers do use it to add a kick to something they're selling, but it is used in hospitals as a painkiller, especially for cancer patients, and as anesthesia in some cases. Almost always as a patch or through an IV, never in pills."

"I don't understand."

'There was a bottle of pills in your husband's possession, pills laced with a heavy dose of fentanyl. That's why we're suspicious."

It took her a moment to absorb it. She grabbed a tissue from a box beside her and blew her nose. She looked directly at Thompson and cocked her head slightly. 'I still don't understand. That doesn't make sense, does it?"

"No, Ma'am. It doesn't. Not if it was suicide."

Mac watched her closely, looking for any emotion beyond sorrow and confusion, something that might be exposed by downturned eyes, a tremor, a swallow, or a change in body posture. But she betrayed nothing except the grief and uncertainty of a woman who had just unexpectedly lost her husband, her hands in her lap still clutching the tissue.

Thompson continued. "If he killed himself with fentanyl, why not just take it? There was no reason to dose the pills. You said he kept a bottle of painkillers here. Do you know if they're still here?"

She immediately popped out of the chair and moved toward the kitchen. "Yes, I saw them this morning. He keeps them…kept them…. on the upper shelf by the stove."

She opened a cabinet, stood on her toes, and started to reach for a small pill bottle when she stopped and turned back to the men. "I probably shouldn't touch that, should I?"

Mac was already standing behind her. "No, Ma'am. Let me get them." He took two paper towels from a roll on the counter and took the bottle by the cap.

"Do you have a plastic bag – like a sandwich bag or something?"

She rifled through a drawer and handed him a zippered bag.

"We'll have to test these." He held the small tube up to the light and saw a half dozen yellow pills that looked like oxycodone.

"I know this is a hard time, but we have a few more questions." He led her back to the family room.

Thompson leaned forward now. "Do you know anyone that would want to harm your husband… anyone he quarreled with… anyone at work or in the neighborhood?"

She shook her head and did not hesitate. "No one. Sheriff, Evan was as meek as they come. He avoided arguments, conflicts. I don't know if everyone liked him but I do know that there was nobody that disliked him enough to do something like that."

"Did he have any close friends…someone we could talk to?"

"Not really. He had a couple of high school buddies still around here, but they rarely got together. There were a few at the hospital, but they were work friends. They didn't hang out together. Evan wasn't much of a socializer. He spent the weekends at his parents' farm and sometimes took the kids fishing. That was about it."

Thompson moved on. "How was your financial situation?"

"Oh, fine. I mean, everybody has to deal with money issues, but we both made good money, and it's been better lately. I think Evan got a raise a few months ago."

Mac raised his eyebrows. "You think?"

For the first time, she seemed unsure. "Evan didn't like to talk about money. It seemed like it always ended in an argument. We kept separate bank accounts. He paid the bills and made the investments. I made my car payment and bought my personal things. When I asked, he just said he got a small raise but never said how much. I didn't ask anything else."

Mac nodded and looked around the room. "Would he have kept any money around the house? Do you have a safe or a place where you keep emergency cash?"

He saw her fidget and cross her legs underneath her in the chair.

"No, I don't think so. I think he would have told me. We don't have a safe."

Thompson waited for a moment and then looked at her. "Ms. Winter, do you own a gun?"

Her mind raced. She was confused and didn't like the way the conversation was turning. She paused to add caution to her words. "We have a pistol."

"What kind and where do you keep it?"

"Sheriff, I don't know anything about guns. We bought it a few months ago. Evan said he wanted to have something around the house for protection. He also has an old rifle of some kind and a shotgun he took to the farm sometimes." She took a long drink of the soda and wiped the sweat from the glass with the palm of her hand. "Why are you asking about guns? What does that have to do with anything?"

"Probably nothing, but we'd like to see it if possible."

She steered them to the bedroom and pointed. "It's in there, top drawer of the nightstand. We never used it. It's still in the box it came in."

Mac opened the drawer and pulled out an oblong plastic box stamped "Ruger" across the top. Based on its weight, he knew the pistol was not there. He set it on the bed and opened it. All it contained was a cheap trigger lock and an owner's manual.

Lucy seemed genuinely surprised. "I don't know; we always kept it there."

***

For the next hour, Lucy answered questions about the gun. Had she ever fired it? When was the last time she saw the gun? Could he have taken it to the farm? Why was it registered in her name? Was there anyone with access to their home who could have taken it? That question had made her uneasy.

Although uncertain, she gave the men permission to help her search the house. They checked the other nightstand, under the mattress, and in the master closet. Her heart leaped into her throat when Mac rattled the shoebox on the top shelf that, until a few days ago, had held an unexplainable amount of cash.

In a last effort, they searched the garage before leaving. As they stood just inside the open garage door, she asked again, "I don't understand. Evan died of a drug overdose. Why is the gun important?"

Mac and Thompson looked at each other, and Mac allowed Thompson to take the question. "It may not have anything to do with anything. We're just covering all the bases."

He looked at her as she stood with her arms folded, sweat beading on her forehead and around her neck before they walked outside the garage.

After an internal debate, he said, "It's highly possible that your husband was murdered. There are two other murders that may be connected, and they were both killed by a gun of the same caliber as yours."

She was now stunned, standing silently.

"Please keep looking, and if you find it, call us immediately. If you don't find it tomorrow, I recommend that you file a report with Seymore PD. It would probably be in your best interest."

She closed the garage door and returned to the house as they drove away. "Damn, Damn, Damn." She uttered under her breath.

She stood by the kitchen counter, grabbed her phone, and dialed. Again, it went straight to voicemail, but this time, she left a message, "Louis, something bad is going on; I really need to talk to you. Please. Please call me."

As she laid the phone down, her emotions and thoughts were jumbled. She stood for a long time, staring at the empty gun case now sitting on the counter. Her mind moved to a time in January when Evan had been out of town, her indiscretion, her night of childish passion with Louis Rich in the bed she shared with her husband. If Evan hadn't taken the pistol, could it have been Louis Rich?

CHAPTER 34

He almost smiled when he saw it – an actual Coke in a glass bottle on the bottom shelf of the store cooler. Up the aisle to the checkout, he grabbed a small bag of salted nuts and placed both on the counter.

Once in the car, he cranked it to turn on the air conditioning before twisting off the cap and pouring the nuts into the bottle. It was one of the few redneck pleasures he had taken to, taught to him by his uncle, his mother's little brother, on his rare summer visits to Gadsden. He turned up the bottle, the salty sweetness hitting the back of his throat, a few nuts filtered to his tongue.

He told himself that the weekend in the casino in Tunica had created a barrier between his life in Seymore and what was ahead. He had drunk too much, gambled too much, and eaten too much, which was not his habit.

He had limited success with a woman from Little Rock, who was obviously married and seeking to learn if she was still attractive to the opposite sex after fifteen years of laundry and little league games. It never passed beyond the flirting and petting stage.

He'd lost over two thousand dollars of Lucy's money at the blackjack tables with no regrets. He still had nearly seventeen thousand wrapped with a rubber band stashed in the console and his own funds in a small case in the trunk.

Things had gone as well as he could expect. He had made two nightly trips from Seymore with his most prized possessions, and now, the last of his clothes and a few odds and ends were stowed in the car.

He did regret the loss of his furniture and the big screen he had only purchased a few months before, but he had managed to sell them for twenty cents on the dollar to the couple in the neighboring condo.

He was clean – no remaining baggage, no paper trail, no loose ends except for Fugly Brown, and he'd just have to live with that one. Any remaining bills were on autopay, but he had only left enough funds to keep the account open.

They would set him up with a new identity, make him an errand boy for a while until things cooled off and he'd be back in business by the end of the year.

He pulled around the gas pumps and out of the parking lot to the ramp to I-55. It was a fifteen-minute drive before he exited onto Highway 51 and soon entered an industrial area. He pulled into a fenced storage facility, punched in a code, and found his unit before unloading the cash and a half dozen boxes.

He exited north and drove only a few blocks. The warehouse was old and ugly, marked with dents from forklifts and tractor trailers, rust, and peeling paint. There was no signage and no outside activity. He pulled in front of an overhead door and blew his horn twice. Almost immediately, the overhead rolled open, and he pulled inside, the door closing behind him.

CHAPTER 35

Fugly Brown's bravado was gone this time; his slack-jawed arrogance had evaporated, replaced by a wavering chin and uncertain eyes. He sat still and hunched, his ever-present cap in his lap.

"Ok, Fugly, what you got for me?" Thompson stood behind him in the doorway to his office.

Fugly looked across the empty desk and never turned toward the Sheriff so that he wouldn't have to look him in the eye and told the story he had rehearsed all morning. "I been trying to remember stuff since we talked, Sheriff. Something came to me over the weekend, something that Deeter said. I knew he had to be selling something cause he always had a little money. Deeter just grinned when I asked him about it. He said he didn't want to talk about it, but then again, you could tell that he did – kinda wanted to brag about it. He said there was a rich man who could get him a steady supply. I didn't ask – a supply of what."

Thompson said, "Uh huh, go on."

"Well, after I remembered that, I got to thinking. That didn't sound like Deeter, talking bout a "rich" man. The way he said it just didn't sound right. So, I'm thinking, that might have been the man's name, not necessarily that he had a lot of money. The more I think about it, the more I think that's right."

"And you just now remembered this, huh?" Thompson walked into the room and sat behind the desk so he could see Fugly's eyes.

"Yes, sir." He looked up at Thompson but couldn't hold the stare. His eyes returned to his lap. "I mean, it was a while ago, and finding out about my kid and all and knowing I got jail time coming, it just kind of slipped my mind."

Thompson picked up the office phone and punched a button. "Mac, could you come in here?"

Mac exited the conference room where he had been updating Dolan and Smith about Lucy Winter's missing gun, and now he stood in the doorway, surprised to see Fugly.

Thompson said, "I take it that you know Louis Rich."

Fugly tried to look surprised. "Sheriff, I've been racking my brain, but as far as I know, I don't know anybody named Rich."

Mac spoke over his shoulder. "You ever go to the free clinic, Fugly?"

"Sure, I've been there a few times."

"But you don't know Louis Rich?"

He shook his head. "Who's Louis Rich?"

"He's the nurse practitioner at the clinic. He knows you."

Fugly smiled and turned to Mac, nodding his head agreeably. "Sure. He's the young guy with the fifty-dollar haircut, but I never knew his name. It's not like I had to write him a check or something. We never had much of a conversation. Seemed like he always looked down his nose at me. So that's Louis Rich."

"He said you had been there a few times. I believe the last time for some kind of rash?"

Fugly hesitated now, not wanting to step into the middle of a lie. Finally, he said, "Yeah, that's right."

Thompson wheeled his chair back from the desk and stretched his arms over his head. He looked at the man for a moment before pulling a cigarette from the pack in his pocket and tapping it against the back of his hand.

"Fugly, you are a piece of work." He stared at him. "You got anything else that you just happened to remember?"

"No, sir."

"Well, get on outta here then."

As he rose, he put the stained cap back on his head and looked from one man to the other. "Sheriff, you gonna help me out with my time?"

"I ain't decided yet, Fugly. By the way, how's that rash doing?"

Fugly just smiled and rubbed his crotch. "Fine, all gone away now."

***

As they sat on the benches outside the courthouse so that Thompson could smoke, Mac watched as he pulled an old tarnished lighter from his pocket and flicked it a few times before it lit.

"Where'd you get that?"

Thompson held it in his palm and looked at it. "Lost mine a while back. This was my Dad's. He carried it for two years in Vietnam. About the only thing he left me. Almost forgot I had it." He took a long draw and looked at Mac. "What do you think?"

"It fits. Looks like it's time to have a talk with Mr. Rich." He laughed lightly.

Thompson looked at him curiously and said, "What?"

"How many fellas like Fugly Brown you reckon we got in this town? More than we need, I guess. He can't tell the truth without wrapping it in a lie."

CHAPTER 36

"So, you haven't seen him since last Thursday?"

Ed Lang's face showed concern as he flopped back into his chair after greeting Thompson and Mac. "He came in at three o'clock on Thursday, handed me his badge, and said since he had two weeks' vacation coming, to consider it his two-week notice. It came as a complete surprise. We had no hint he was even considering another job. You kinda expect that from hourly employees but not a medical professional."

"Where's this other job?"

"We don't know. Louis wouldn't tell me. He just said he had taken another position, but the paperwork wasn't signed yet, and he didn't feel that he could disclose that."

Lang's anger was evident, and now his curiosity. "He left us in a significant bind. We're scrambling now to find someone to cover his shifts. Why are you looking for him?"

Thompson said, "We have some questions relevant to our investigations. Could you pull his file so we can verify his contact information, maybe find an emergency contact?"

Lang grabbed a file from the top of a stack on his desk. "Got it right here. I'll have my secretary make a copy for you." He looked intently at Thompson. "I got your warrant from our attorney this morning. Does it have anything to do with that?"

Thompson evaded the question with one of his own. "How well do you know Rich?"

"I didn't know him socially, only through the hospital. He was a good worker, usually cheerful, and quick to help or volunteer. He was our best worker at the free clinic."

Lang had buzzed the secretary, who now stood dutifully in the doorway. "Make two copies of this file and give them to the Sheriff."

The young man looked surprised. "The whole file?"

"Everything."

Lang turned back to Thompson and Mac. "We want to cooperate with you in any way that we can. I've already instructed our financial officer to make copies of the pharmacy records. You should have them sometime tomorrow."

Lang looked sorrowful and defeated, his usual polished demeanor tarnished. "This is a hell of a mess. Now, I've got to replace a pharmacist and a nurse practitioner. Those aren't easy to find, not for a small hospital like ours. Sheriff, I've got a lot of questions, and I've got to answer a lot of questions. My board's called an emergency meeting for this evening, and I have nothing to tell them. Is there anything you can tell me?"

Thompson almost felt sympathy for the man and questioned if he had misjudged him. "Not much. You can tell them this; We are still investigating Evan Winter's death, and a review of his records is part of that investigation. We will be as discreet as possible, but you know your staff will see what's happening. I've got no control over what they may say or think. As far as Louis Rich is concerned, we just want to ask him some questions about Winter and some things we've discovered about the free clinic. If you hear from him, please contact us immediately."

Lang rose and walked into the outer office with Thompson and Mac. He took the copies of Rich's personnel file from the secretary's desk and handed them to Thompson.

"I'll personally bring the hospital records to your office in the morning."

He watched the men leave before turning to the young man behind the desk. "Contact all departments. No one is to leave at shift change until we have a staff meeting."

***

Weeks of investigation had now turned into a paper shuffle. By Tuesday morning, piles of files and financial records made their way to Thompson's desk. A review of Rich's personnel file yielded items of interest but little value.

His emergency contact number proved to be his mother, a mother that he had previously indicated was deceased. The number was out of service. He had left no forwarding address, and a check with the postal service did not indicate that a hold or a forwarding address order had been applied for.

As the heat of summer reached its height, the days dragged on, filled with an endless stream of paperwork and phone calls. A statewide BOLO had been issued for Rich without result. Smith and Dolan had resorted to contacting small hospitals, clinics, and the three big hospital systems in the state, looking for Rich or someone who fit his description. The man had simply vanished.

Thompson's frustration had reached a boiling point. Heated exchanges with the District Attorney and political posturing by local powerbrokers seeking to protect the hospital and the community's reputation had done little to improve his mood.

The investigation turned in all directions. The prescription pad in Dean's possession had little to offer that wasn't expected. It obviously had come from the free clinic, but no one assumed responsibility for its loss, along with two other pads. Rich became an easy scapegoat, and that was about as far as it had gone.

The examination of Winter's death was at a standstill. Without a clear manner of death, there was little more that could be done except around the edges as it related to the pharmacy.

Lucy Winter held some key to the whole thing. He was sure of it. Mac had interviewed her twice since their initial visit, and while she seemed cooperative, he felt she was hiding something.

She was startled when Mac asked her about Louis Rich. She admitted that Evan and Rich were casual friends, had a close working relationship, and that Rich had been in their home on several occasions. When asked if she thought it was a possibility that Rich had taken the Ruger from their home, her response was, "I don't know; I suppose it's possible."

In the last interview, she disclosed that she was negotiating a teaching contract in Pontotoc County to be closer to her family. The school year started in only a few weeks, and the house was already on the market.

The interviews continued: hospital personnel, free clinic workers, local pharmacists, and Evan Winter's parents, who were distraught at the upcoming loss of daily visits with their grandchildren.

The records from the hospital pharmacy and the free clinic presented a different set of problems. Mac and Thompson had personally poured over the documents. They could read them and understand the basic accounting, but without some basis of comparison with a knowledge they did not have, there was no way to determine if there were any discrepancies or evidence of wrongdoing.

Thompson spent a whole day on a trip to Jackson, negotiating an agreement with a qualified CPA to examine the documents. The county supervisors had authorized up to ten thousand dollars for the audit. They had reached an agreement at seventy-five hundred and Thompson piled the file boxes on a worktable in a third-floor office in downtown Jackson, returning with a receipt and a promise of results within two weeks.

With little left to investigate, he returned Dolan and Smith to regular duty, and Mac worked on an "as-needed" basis.

The stress of the last few weeks had wreaked havoc on Thompson's health. Adjusting his medication was problematic. On two occasions, his blood sugar had dropped into the danger zone, causing a near collapse. He had taken to carrying a pack of peanut butter crackers in his pocket.

It was six on a Thursday evening. The office was deserted except for two 911 dispatchers in a control room at the far end of the hall. Elam Thompson stared at the fast-food burger and fries on his desk. The grease from the burger had begun to soak through the wrapper, leaving a small moon of moisture on the desktop when he picked it up. Out of the corner of his eye, he caught the framed picture on the wall, a photo he saw every day. He paused and then said aloud to himself, "Hell... this ain't gonna be easy, is it?"

He tossed the burger in the trash can beside his desk and swept the fries and ketchup packets into it as well. He pulled his cell from his pocket and dialed. "Mac, you still going fishing this weekend?"

CHAPTER 37

Mac pulled into the cracked and crumbling driveway. His eyes were at once drawn to the "For Sale" sign in the yard of the house next door and the young couple standing on the lawn with a local realtor. He smiled and nodded before walking up the drive.

Sweet met him at the door. "I sure do appreciate this, Mr. Mac." She handed him a square box of lightbulbs and pointed him toward the hall. "I'll be glad to pay you for your time."

"Well, as a matter of fact, you can. A cup of coffee sounds pretty good – once I get through."

Mac changed a handful of bulbs and took the trash to the bin by the street before sitting at the kitchen table. A steaming cup was waiting for him.

He looked at the tiny dog peering around the corner of the counter, a low growl emanating from a trembling mouth. "How's Toot doing?"

"He's doin'." An exaggerated scowl on her face. "He's the beggin'est dog I ever seen. Arlene gave him people food. I won't do that, but he's getting used to it. His farts ain't so bad anymore, but Lawd, I can't sit down fer him. Always wantin' to be in my lap."

He smiled and looked toward the dog again. "I guess that's why they call them "lap dogs."

Sweet just grunted and added more coffee to Mac's cup.

He looked around the room for any other chores that might need to be done before saying, "I see Ms. Deeter's house is up for sale."

"Yes, sir, since they put her in the nursing home, they got to have some money. She never had no money, just that house and a few acres of land out west of town. They gonna sell that too. Them Medicaid folks don't play."

"Maybe you'll get some good neighbors. There's a young couple over there now."

"They black or white?"

"They're a black couple. Is that important to you?"

"I don't reckon. Just wanted to know." She seemed slightly embarrassed.

She turned toward him as if to gauge his reaction to what she was about to say. "What happened to Arlene, got me to thinkin'. I ain't never really put my affairs in order. I got some burial insurance, so that's taken care of, but there are other things." She paused and spooned more coffee into the saucer to cool. "I was wondering… if it ain't too much trouble. If I ain't asking too much…" she paused again.

He smiled at her and gripped his cup. "Go ahead, ask. All I can say is yes or no."

"I ain't got no family left – outlived em all. There's some good folks at the church, but I don't want no squabbling, and I done heard that making an attorney your executor ain't the best idea. Would you do it for me?"

He hesitated only a moment. "Of course. I'll be glad to, but you know you'll still need an attorney to draw it all up."

She smiled. "Already took care of that. Your wife took me to one this morning."

He laughed. "I should have known."

She blew over the saucer, and Mac saw the tightness and tension leave her face. "I want you to know exactly what you're getting into."

He nodded but said, "You don't have to tell me anything."

She shook her head. "I don't wanna go to no nursing home if I can help it. Rather be at home with some help. I had him draw up a power of attorney with your name on it. I'll keep it in a file box in my bedroom till you need it. I figure you'll do right by me."

"Yes, ma'am, I'll do my best. Can you afford that if the time comes?"

"I got this house; it's paid for, and there's a quarter section of land north of town. My papa left that to me a long time ago. Fella told me the timber would be ready to cut in a year or two. The deeds are in that file box, too."

She reached over and took his hand in hers, her fingers still strong and strangely beautiful with age. "I got 240,000 dollars in accounts at the bank. Only good thing about being old. There ain't much you want and even less to spend it on."

He looked into her eyes and saw a light that was rare in people her age. "Yes, ma'am."

She continued, "The house and the land are going to the church. They can do what they want with them. But any money that's left over… I got something in mind but I'm not sure how to do it. I may need your help."

He waited without responding.

"I been livin here all my life. Just about everybody around here ain't got no money. I don't reckon the county's got much money either, and I been lookin around at all the things we ain't got. There's stray dogs and cats all over the place. I don't like thinkin about what happens to em. There ain't much of an animal shelter here. You may think I'm crazy, but I wanna use that money to start one. They can even put my name on it if they want." She looked at him over the top of her glasses.

"That sounds fine, Sweet. That sounds just fine." He smiled and marveled at the old woman.

Mac sat in his truck in Sweet's driveway, shook his head, and smiled again. He dialed Mary. "I'll be home in about twenty minutes. I see you've been busy today. We'll have to discuss what you got me into."

CHAPTER 38

Mac walked into the office for the first time in a week. Since the investigation had slowed and with budget considerations, he now only attended a weekly meeting to catch up on any developments and then work if he was needed. He had caught up on his gardening and even got in a round of golf during the previous week.

There had been a few phone calls, questions, and recommendations, but with nearly forty years in law enforcement, he had learned to put a case aside, let it ripen, to mature until the pieces fell into place.

He took his usual place at the conference table along with Dolan and Jimmy and waited for Thompson, who was still on the phone in his office. Jimmy rose and refilled coffee for each of them as Dolan extracted a second pastry from the box on the table.

"Ya'll been catching up?" asked Thompson as he entered the room. He eyed the sweets before sitting at the head of the table.

"Waiting on you, Boss," said Dolan.

"Well, let's bring Mac up to speed." Thompson dropped a small pile of folders on the table and opened the top one.

"Still nothing on Rich's location. The man just disappeared. His cell is no longer in service. I think we've checked every hospital, clinic, and private doc in the state, and there's been no recent hires of anyone that fits his description."

"We checked his employment history that he provided to the hospital. The last place he claimed to work – never heard of him. Their phone number on his resume didn't match the hospital's personnel office."

Mac whistled. "That's not good; that's not good at all. What did Lang say about that?"

"What could he say? He just thanked me for the info and said he'd check it out. Pretty sure he knows it could cost him his job."

Dolan said, "You'd think they would've done a thorough background on him for an important job like that."

Mac responded, " In a small hospital like this, if a guy comes in with an impressive resume, they probably hire him on the spot. I'm sure they intended to follow up, but by all accounts, he was doing a good job, and sometimes you don't want to know what you don't know."

Thompson said, "Mac, you told me that he claimed to graduate from the University of Memphis, so I contacted them, explained the situation, and they sent me photos of all the male graduates from their program. We limited it to white males over a reasonable five-year time period."

Thompson pulled a stack of papers from the folder and pushed them toward the investigator. "I realized I had never met the man; I just saw his picture in his personnel file. Look through those and see if you see him."

Mac began to shuffle through the pages as Thompson continued. "We've almost completed a check of the free clinic's records against the local pharmacists. We're looking at a few in neighboring counties and Coyville. What we've found is pretty interesting."

Mac pulled a page from the records and set it aside before continuing to review the remaining stack. He looked up at Thompson. "Let me guess. There's a hell of a lot more prescriptions than indicated by the clinic's books."

Thompson nodded. "Nearly a hundred more from February till mid-June. They stopped about the time of Dean and Deeter's murders. All for narcotics, mostly hydrocodone, oxycodone, Dilaudid, and some alprazolam. We're still sorting through them to separate those that look legitimate from those that aren't."

Mac returned to the page he set aside before tapping it with his finger. "That's him. The haircut's different, and he's obviously older now, but that's him. Thomas Renfeld." He leaned across the table and pushed the photograph to Thompson.

Elam looked at the image and smiled before handing it to Jimmy Smith. "Now we've got something. Just to be sure, let's make a few copies and take them to Lang and some hospital staff for verification. Maybe, have Lucy Winter take a look. I'd like to see her reaction."

Dolan looked at the photo and said, "We can file charges now, right? Maybe identity theft?"

"Maybe," said Mac. "That's if Louis Rich was a real person. But more importantly, we got him for fraud, forgery, and probably a few more things. We'll have to look into it."

Thompson said, "I need all of you back on this full-time. Let's get an arrest warrant filed for Rich, aka Renfeld, and add it to the BOLO that's already out on him. Dolan, contact Memphis PD and the Shelby County Sheriff's Office and give them the particulars. Mac, if you would contact the University and see what you can find out about Thomas Renfeld... and Jimmy, take a couple of copies of that photo to the hospital and show it around. See if Lang and a few others agree that's Louis Rich."

Mac pulled off his glasses and cleaned them with a handkerchief he pulled from his pocket. "None of this is helping us with the Winter case. Where are we on the hospital pharmacy records?"

"It'll be a couple more days before we get the full report, but I spoke with the CPA yesterday. The preliminary review shows a couple of things. An inordinate amount of out-of-date drugs was destroyed over the last few months, more than would be typical for a small hospital. Winter and Rich signed off on all of them since last September. He said it also appeared that some of the invoices may have been altered. He's contacted the drug companies to get a copy of their records."

They sat in silence for a few moments, absorbing all the information. Mac was the first to speak. "There's a lot of evidence, and it all points in one direction, but it is mostly circumstantial. We can't nail him to the wall with what we got."

Smith had been quietly listening and now spoke. "I can't help but wonder why this Renfeld would use a false name. If he were a legitimate nurse practitioner, why would he do that?"

"Probably because he's done it before and got caught. Might have even done time."

The briefing was the first time Thompson had laid out all the evidence accumulated in the past few days. It brought a rush of excitement and hopefulness. "I'm calling MIB and seeing if they can help us with all the out-of-state stuff. They'll get more cooperation than we can. Maybe there's an arrest record on Renfeld in Tennessee."

Thompson closed the open file in front of him and stood. "Alright, let's get going. We'll meet back here at four."

***

Thompson spent the next hour on the phone with Jesse Deitrich. In between excuses and some heavy-handed advice on how to properly handle his investigation, he was able to extract a promise of cooperation. MIB would work with Tennessee authorities on any arrest records or any other information that could be found on Thomas Renfeld. Deitrich also agreed to help extend the BOLO into Tennessee.

By the time he hung up the phone, his throat was dry, his voice was coarse. He headed to the breakroom and considered coffee but opted for a diet soda and a glass of ice.

Lindon leaned into the doorway. "Boss, you had a call while you were on the line with MIB. The Sheriff in Tunica County wants you to call him back. Said it had to do with a missing person."

He handed him a slip of paper with a phone number.

***

"You got anybody missing down that way?" The voice on the line was high-pitched and nasal.

"I do. At least somebody on the run. Tell me you got somebody I need to come get."

"Well, I don't know about that." There was a long pause. "I guess I better explain. A week ago, we pulled a body out of the river. It had been there a few days, washed up in some debris along the bank in a bend. Pretty bad shape; we couldn't get a good set of fingerprints, no ID, and no missing persons reports that we could match. He's been cooling in our morgue. White male, probably in his thirties or forties- hard to tell sometimes when they've been in the water for a while."

"Dark brown hair, about five-ten?"

"That sounds about right. He had a few bruises but no definitive cause of death. Our coroner says he didn't drown. He was already dead when he hit the water. Anyway, without anybody claiming the body, the coroner was prepping him for long term storage when he went through his clothes again."

Another long pause. "My boys messed up. When they didn't find a wallet, they didn't check his back pockets close enough. I can't blame them too much. I mean, he was kind of a mess. A Mississippi driver's license was tucked in there- almost like somebody stuck it in there after taking his wallet. It was issued to a Louis Rich, address in your town of Seymore. Is that your man?"

Thompson looked at the clock on the wall and the pile of papers on his desk before running his hands through his short, cropped hair. "If you haven't already, you might want to run a full tox screen on him."

"And just exactly what would we be looking for?"

"My guess - fentanyl. If I leave now, I can be there before five. Is that alright?"

CHAPTER 39

It was late morning. The dew on the grass strip between the sidewalk and the parking lot was now dissipated, and the pavement was already too hot for bare feet when Fugly Brown pulled the car in front of the twenty-foot security fence surrounding the hulk of a building.

He stepped to the rear of the car, dressed in sweatpants, a t-shirt, and flip-flops that he would use as shower shoes for the foreseeable future. He felt naked without the cap that now sat on the front seat.

The girl handed the baby to him. He held the child close and swayed nervously back and forth from one foot to the other. He cooed to the boy and kissed him on the forehead.

"You got your money?"

He nodded. "Two hundred dollars, that's all they'll let me have at one time. Should last me for a while since I can't buy cigarettes in there."

He looked down at the girl, nearly a foot shorter than him. Taking her chin in his hand, he held her gaze. "You gonna visit me?"

She nodded. "Every time I can. They've got me on Saturday shift, so it'll have to be on Wednesdays, but I'll be here." She caught herself. "We'll be here if you want us."

He looked up at the sky and the purple thunderhead building far to the west. "Looks like it's gonna rain again this afternoon."

She didn't answer. She took the child from his arms and kissed him softly. "You be careful in there and stay out of trouble. Don't piss off that sheriff, or he'll change his mind and get you sent off to Parchman. I can't hardly visit you there."

He smiled—almost a smirk—as if his arrogance would give him courage. "You gonna pray for me?"

"Fugly, I been praying for you for a long time. Believe it or not, there's a few other folks, too."

His smile vanished, his lips trembled slightly, and his eyes moistened. He turned away from her and looked back at the sky to regain his composure.

"I read something in one of your books, one of them church books you got lying around. I've been thinking about it a lot, but I'm not sure what to make of it."

She looked up at him, waiting for him to continue, the baby now on her hip.

"It was more like a question. It said something about how come folks ain't praying for Satan. I'm like, my God, who in thousands of years ever thought to pray for the devil his own self? I guess that's something for me to think on."

He turned and walked up the sidewalk until he reached the heavy metal door and pressed a button on the wall. He turned until he faced directly into a security camera and said, "Alan Simpson Brown."

The door buzzed and clicked and then swung open. He walked in, and it slammed shut behind him.

She leaned against the car for a long time, staring at the door and then the approaching clouds before wiping the drool from the teething child's chin.

"You ain't a bad man, Fugly. Just for Christ's sake, understand, you ain't a bad man."

CHAPTER 40

The morning air was crisp for the first time since May, a sure sign that high school football weather would push its way into central Mississippi over the next few weeks, bringing relief from the months of pounding heat and draining humidity.

Mac eased his truck around the green behemoth gobbling up garbage along the streets of Seymore. He waved his fingers at the yellow-vested man standing on the rear bumper, his arm wrapped around a support as the monster rumbled forward to its next stop.

Three blocks ahead, he pulled along the curb in front of a Sheriff's Department truck. He exited and joined Thompson, as they stood together between the two vehicles.

"Lindon told me you might be here. What's going on?"

He pointed at the bob truck and a heavy-duty pickup with an attached trailer parked on a side street. The just unloaded track hoe was slowly crawling across a yard toward an old frame pre-war bungalow.

"Just a little demolition work." He looked at Mac and smiled. "Haven't seen you for a while."

"I had a free morning and had to get out of the house. My garden's about played out, and the fish ain't biting, so I thought I'd catch up."

Thompson stared at the track hoe as it sidled up to the side of the house and said, "Nothing new to tell you. It all died with Rich or Renfeld or whoever the hell he was … and that ain't our case."

His voice stiffened. "But that leaves me with three unresolved murders I'm gonna have to live with."

Mac didn't know what to say. He had no words of wisdom or solace for the younger man. Old, unsettled cases never faded completely from a man's memory, sometimes stealing sleep and peace of mind. What was it he had said? *That backward march of dead pursuits.*

Instead, he turned to the scene in front of him. "That house looks pretty solid, and this is a good neighborhood. Why are they tearing it down?"

They watched as the track hoe advanced on the house and raised its bucket to full height before dropping it onto the asphalt roof, tearing a car-sized hole and ripping away at the closest wall.

"It's been vacant for about five years. Nobody willing to live in it. They finally donated it to the church over there to expand their parking lot."

Thompson saw the curiosity on Mac's face. "I guess you weren't here when it all happened."

He wasn't sure he was up to telling this story. He had told it before, and it had never gotten easier, but now he felt obligated.

"He was a Vietnam vet. I guess his time over there messed him up pretty bad. He didn't have any family left around here, just a sister up in Tennessee that would call and check up on him once in a while."

He paused as the track hoe took another swipe at the roof; the crash and crack of splintered wood mixed with the heavy metal clang of the machine's bucket.

"He never caused any trouble. Lived there for years but never mixed with folks. Just wanted to be left alone - him and that big ol' German Shepherd hardly ever left the house. After a while, nobody thought nothing about him – kinda forgot about him. He didn't bother nobody, and nobody bothered with him. His sister came down one Sunday afternoon to check on him."

Thompson stopped and lit a cigarette, inhaling deeply, hoping the tobacco smoke would kill the imagined smell evoked by the memory he was about to relive.

"He filled the bathtub full of water, dumped a can of food in a dog bowl in the kitchen, laid down on the bed, and blew his brains out. Laid there about six weeks."

He gave Mac a sideways look. "You can imagine what that dog did to survive."

Mac winced and stepped back from the truck, a sour taste in the back of his throat. His thoughts fell to his time in New Orleans; the welfare checks prompted by foul odors coming from the apartment next door, the bloated bodies of junkies behind dumpsters in back alleys, the dismembered remains of a woman stuffed in a fifty-gallon drum at an industrial site down by the river.

They stood and watched as the last of the standing walls of the house collapsed into a pile of rubble, a cloud of powdered plaster and dust rising above.

"The thing about it all – now nobody can remember what he looked like – his face, how old he was, the way he carried himself. Nobody cares about what he done, his service in Vietnam or the suffering he must have gone through. They just remember how he died and that awful scene they all imagine. They'll talk about it for years, long after they forget his name."

Thompson grew quiet, then straightened and placed his hands in the small of his back, the cigarette with a long ash still in his mouth.

"What happened to the dog?"

Thompson pulled the cigarette and thumped the ash to the ground. He looked back up the street, watching the garbage truck and the men scurrying back and forth across the pavement with plastic bins in tow.

"Hell of a time we live in, ain't it?" He seemed to momentarily lose himself in his own thoughts. "My little girl starts kindergarten next week. They have to grow up too fast. It won't be long before she's gonna be out in this world where I know I can't keep her safe."

Mac leaned against the truck and clasped his hands over the hood. "That's just the price we pay for having kids. When my son was born, someone told me that I'd never sleep sound again. He was right. Now, you have this precious thing you never had before, and every fine day is wrapped in fear. When they're little, it's not so hard. Yeah, you worry, but you're there. You can try to teach them, paddle them when they're bad, hold them close. But as they start to grow up, they're damned determined to find their own way in this world, and you can't stop them. You lose control. You can't always protect them anymore. Ain't a damned thing you can do about it but pray on it."

Elam tossed the cigarette into the curb and spat between his feet, not looking up.

"Nobody knew what to do with that dog. I mean, it was a god-awful thing, but it wasn't the dog's fault. He just wanted to survive—and you had to wonder if it changed him like it would a person. I don't know. Nobody blamed the dog, but nobody wanted it either—to be reminded of what he done."

He gave Mac a tired smile, walked to the truck's door, lifted the door latch, and waited for the growling garbage truck to move on to the next block.

"I guess we've got laws for just about everything now. If we ain't got one, we just twist one till it fits. But sometimes things just happen– things so awful we can't imagine that we'd ever need a law for them; things so bad, so gut-wrenching - we can't deal with them. Ain't no law worth a damn for those things."

"I don't want to talk about that dog."

ALSO BY W. W. MCCULLY

Murder in Rural Hill

Bones of Mississippi

The Tragedy of Janie Sharp

Made in the USA
Columbia, SC
04 July 2024

c203aa6b-6416-4d1a-ae28-07eb3e8e6042R01